Ian Watson was born on Tyneside in 1943. He studied English at Balliol College, Oxford. His first speculative fiction stories were stimulated by his three-year stay as a lecturer in Japan. In 1969 *Roof Garden Under Saturn*, a short story, was published in *New Worlds* magazine, and since then his stories have appeared in various magazines and anthologies. They have also been published in book form in two collections, *The Very Slow Time Machine* and *Sunstroke*.

Ian Watson's first novel, *The Embedding*, was published in 1973 and received enormous critical acclaim. His second novel, *The Jonah Kit*, became a British Science Fiction Award winner as well as confirming his position in the front rank of contemporary British writers. He has been features editor of the journal *Foundation* since 1975 and a full-time writer since 1976.

By the same author

The Embedding
The Jonah Kit
The Martian Inca
Alien Embassy
Miracle Visitors
The Very Slow Time Machine
God's World
The Gardens of Delight
Deathhunter
Sunstroke
Chekhov's Journey
The Book of the River

IAN WATSON

Converts

PANTHER
Granada Publishing

Panther Books
Granada Publishing Ltd
8 Grafton Street, London W1X 3LA

First published by Panther Books 1984

Author's Note
Parts of this novel appeared in different form
as a story 'Jean Sandwich, the Sponsor and I'
in *Universe 11* edited by Terry Carr.

ISBN 0-586-05895-8

Reproduced, printed and bound in Great Britain by
Hazell Watson & Viney Limited, Aylesbury, Bucks

Set in Plantin

To John, Greta and Anna Power

Contents

PART ONE
Geneva

Chapter 1

'Jean Sandwich?'

Frank Caldero struck a casual pose in front of the surveillance camera. Mounted over the elevator door, this was the only camera in the whole lobby. Nor was this the only shortcoming about the security system of Paradise Apartments. A big black mark must equally be awarded to the tangle of Swiss Cheese plants choking one wall. Doubtless these plants helped to maintain the pretence of Paradise; but any human snake could lurk in ambush there.

These minor observations merely served to confirm what Frank already knew in some detail about the economic status of the woman he was visiting. She was on the borderline, between Eden and the jungle.

'Jean Sandwich? Jean Sandra Norwich?'

'Yes, who is that?'

The intercom box made the woman's voice blurred and crackly: defect number three.

'My name's Frank Caldero, Miz Sandwich.' He produced the bundle of money from his inside pocket and flourished the bank-notes at the camera, fanning them. 'As you can see, I don't intend to burgle you. Far from it! I have a proposition of a rather private nature for you.'

Realizing the lewd possibilities of what he had just said, Frank burst out laughing.

'Oh hell, that sounds completely wrong! What I want, Miz Sandwich, is to pay you – and handsomely too: five thousand, to be exact – just to listen to me for half an hour, then neither to say nor write nor otherwise publicize nor even confide to a friend what I shall propose during the course of that half hour. The money's yours, whether you say yes or no to my subsequent proposals.'

'You sound like a walking legal contract, Mr Caldero . . . Hey, do my ears deceive me? Five thousand, just for listening?'

'That's the general idea. I'm approaching you on·behalf of

someone whom we shall refer to between us as the Sponsor. Though I'd better point out right away that he doesn't sponsor chat shows or anything like that.'

'Why didn't you phone and tell me you were coming?'

'Random phone-taps. Key word sampling by our friendly Government computers. This is a very private affair.'

'Aren't you just a little bit scared, standing there in a public place waving all that money about?' She was playing him along now, studying him.

'It *is* rather public, isn't it? There are much more private places than this. Agree to my proposal, and you'll have the run of the best of them. But I already checked those Swiss Cheeses for any worms hiding in the holes – and I left a couple of friends sitting outside in an armoured limo.'

Maccoby and McKinnon were . . . friends?

Actually, the security chief and his bodyguard buddy were very civil fellows, usually. It was just that Frank never felt particularly comfortable in their presence. Who knew what the Terrible Two had got up to before Bruno King hired them?

Frank corrected himself: before the *Sponsor* hired them . . .

'Are you a plant lover, Mr Caldero?'

'Oh, I'm quite versatile. I can recognize a *Monstera Deliciosa* when I see one.'

'Speaking of private places, I hear the grave's fine and private. You might want to murder me.'

'A fine and private place, but none I think do there embrace.'

'Hey, you're a poetry freak, too! I think I like you.'

'If I wanted to kill you, I'd just hide behind those leaves and wait.'

'You might want to torture me a while, first. You can't do that so easily in a lobby.'

'And thus avenge the ungodly words you write? To redeem, by pain, from Hell's pains? *Per* agony *ad astra*? That might be typical of some rabid God Nut. But frankly – and I'm always Frank – what I shall be proposing on the Sponsor's behalf is distinctly blasphemous in the eyes of the God Nuts. Still, if you're worried, I'll lay a bet you have a gun tucked away up there. We all have to protect our Paradise, don't we? So why don't you just fetch your gun and keep it pointed at me all the time I'm up there talking to you? If my silver eloquence won't sway you, I deserve no better than lead.' Frank pulled what he hoped was a tragi-comic face, recollecting too late that if the camera was equipped with a fish-eye lens this might well distort his expression into a horrid leer.

'I'm offering you five G, just to listen. And if you go through with what I'll propose, whether it's successful or not there's one million for you, to be banked in Zürich in your own name or whichever name you like. I can't say any more down here.'

'Did I just hear you – ?'

'One million.'

'This Sponsor of yours . . .'

'Must be rich. He is.'

'It sounds crazy.'

'No, he just happens to want something very special from you.'

'How can a lady refuse? I'll send the elevator down.'

Within the elevator there was no surveillance camera: defect number four. Had there been a camera, it would have spied a chunky man of middle height with short crinkly black hair, like lamb's wool. He wore horn-rimmed glasses to correct a mild myopia.

Frank sometimes liked to imagine himself as Superman in Clark Kent guise – admittedly a reduced version. For though he lacked the necessary height and physique, even of Clark Kent, he did dispense some of the power of Superman, courtesy of the Sponsor. (Whilst Bruno King looked even less like either Superman or Clark Kent; but he meant to do something about this. Soon, too.)

However, Frank knew perfectly well that he would never launch himself into the sky, and fly. At heart he was too earth-bound. As solidly rooted as a tree.

Frank's nose twitched in a rabbity fashion as he reseated his glasses. As the elevator rose laboriously up the shaft, he dismissed his own fantasies and concentrated on Jean instead.

Chapter 2

Jean Sandwich wasn't her real name. Before she married Mike Hoffman – now firmly divorced – her name had been Jean Sandra Norwich. In bitter humour at her situation, she had run her last two names together.

She might have made the point even plainer by altering the spelling of her first name to 'Gene': *Gene Sandwich*. But that would have introduced a note of sexual ambiguity. Whereas Jean wasn't in the least ambiguous about her sex – or about the fact that Sex, in the broadest definition of the term, had done her in. Sex had hogtied her. Sex had condemned her to a ludicrous fate.

No ordinary annoyance at sexual role-typing inspired her change of name, however. It was something far more biologically basic than that. A scientist once declared: 'A human being is merely a means used by a gene, to manufacture another gene.' And like a comic book heroine whirling around to strip off her everyday disguise and reveal her secret powers – or in this case, secret curse – Jean Sandra Norwich became: a gene sandwich. She was the slice of meat imprisoned between the genes of her mother Josie and the genes of her daughter Alison.

It was a life sentence.

Jean went where she pleased, and did what she chose, and showed all the signs of leading a uniquely special, precious existence, full of free will. But she knew in her heart that this was all an illusion.

For she was sandwiched. Those devil genes had laid down the law in daughter Alison, exactly as they had in mother Josie.

Jean had been fiercely sure that she was a huge improvement upon mother Josie – until Alison began to grow up. Jean had been certain that she had pulled herself up successfully by her own bootstraps – until her own stupid mother was recreated, out of Jean's own womb.

The genes cared not a sparrow's fart for the person of beauty and wit whom Jean had made of herself. They spat on her sensitivity and creativity. They pissed on the pottery she crafted to prove her talents: delicate fantasy landscapes full of castles and dragons and giant fungi. The genes preferred the sow's ear to the silk purse any day.

Jean had dreamed that Alison would outshine her by as much again as Jean outshone Josie.

'Foolish machine,' said the genes. And out of Jean there squirmed another animal as lacking in finer feelings as Josie had been. Clearly Alison was destined to run through her whole life as obliviously as her grandmother, like a chicken with its head chopped off.

Maybe the genes sensed how overcrowded the world was getting. Maybe they had decided that sensitivity was out of place. Or perhaps they had foreseen a new ice age or a nuclear war, whereby life would be a matter of grubbing around in the dirt for the next few thousand years. Whatever the truth of this, Jean might be best lean meat, but from now on plain bread seemed to be the staple.

While Alison was still an infant, and hope abounding filled Jean's breast, Jean threw her energies into inscribing love and humour, excellence and artistry upon the slate of her daughter.

Alas, Alison wasn't a slate at all. She was a palimpsest: a twice-used parchment, an economy model. As she grew up, the old writing showed through ever more clearly: the dumb, vandalistic scrawl which denied that there was any special merit to Jean's existence.

In her chagrin, Jean Sandra Hoffman – née Norwich – divorced her husband and became Jean Sandwich.

Yet Jean was far from silent in her disappointment. In a series of virulent magazine articles, which both caught the public's fancy and provoked a counterblast of wrath, she explained in detail why she had walked out on her husband and child, and why uniquely she had sued for non-custody and non-visiting rights.

Unfortunately, her ex-husband Mike tended to agree with her. So there ensued the newsworthy spectacle of the two divorcees fighting in public to off-load responsibility for the product of their love on to the other party. Perhaps because Jean made more commotion, she had won the day. She was more conspicuously unsuited to be a mother, than Mike to be a father.

Yet she had never blamed Mike personally for her horrid spawn and the ruin of her illusions. How could she, when it was her own genes that proved dominant? It was against Nature's deceits that she

13

railed – and how she did rail! She would do anything at all to pay Nature back for the dirty trick played on her.

Consequently one of her articles dealt with the controversial topic of human DNA research. In the very same week that a laboratory believed to be meddling in this field was fire-bombed by a God Nut mob, Jean wrote approving whole-heartedly of anybody who monkeyed around with 'God's blueprints'. (A few days later the magazine office had its windows stoned by a crowd wearing tee-shirts emblazoned with the motto: '*I'm nuts on God*.')

Yet, as Jean pointed out angrily in her article, even if an egg – which she would be glad to donate – were taken from her ovaries to be retailored in a test tube to produce something closer to her heart's desire, all the remaining horde of eggs in her sex organs would still carry the same treacherous message written in them. Not to mention every damn cell in her whole body. Whatever miracles the DNA sculptors worked in their admirable laboratories in China and Japan, she would still remain Jean Sandwich.

The magazine thrived on the wrath. And so did Jean, for a while. Yet the sad truth was that she was already becoming last season's sensation. She was rumoured to be writing a book, but perhaps this was a counsel of desperation.

It was Jean's DNA article which had first caught the Sponsor's eye. Whereupon Frank Caldero had begun checking out Jean's affairs in detail.

It would be an exaggeration to say that the Sponsor had fallen in love with Jean. He was really in love with an idea, with a vision. Jean had simply interposed herself between his eye and that vision.

And now her public profile was fading fast. Which was fine, just fine.

Needless to say, Jean's actual profile – as illustrating her articles – was ample reason for anyone to fall in love with her, thought Frank . . .

Chapter 3

The elevator decanted Frank into another lobby unwatched by any camera eye. Stout apartment doors led off this lobby, with peepholes plugged through them at eye level. Bolted to the door frames were intercom boxes.

Frank pressed the buzzer of apartment 804.

Nothing happened. After waiting for a whole two minutes he banged on the door with his fist.

A chain rattled, and the door swung open.

'Sorry. I forgot. The squawk box up here's bust.' Jean backed away, holding a small pistol, though it was not pointing directly at him. She smiled in apology for the gun and the broken intercom; and her smile devastated him.

Jean had glossy brown eyes, short auburn hair cut in a pageboy trim, and a perfect creamy skin. Her nose was Grecian, her chin firm, and her figure as lovely as ever it had been before her terrible child had swollen it. Her body had never despaired, as other women's bodies might have done. The tragedy was, that lurking in this wonderful body was the genetic government – temporarily in exile – which had swept back to power in her offspring. This splendid Jean was only a sport of Nature: a once-only *Romeo and Juliet* tossed off by the genetic monkey typing pool, which tapped out dumb pulp books all the rest of the time.

Her small lounge was sparsely furnished, though a table in front of the window was buried in house plants. Their foliage completely hid the city outside, silent this Sunday morning. (Nobody was being shot or robbed in the street. No one was rioting. Nothing was burning.) The plants were prisms of Paradise, breaking the white and grey of concrete into green light.

Here were Wandering Jews and ferns and ivies. And fleshy succulents, and bromeliads with pools of water cupped in them. There was a Japanese fan palm. And, lest Jean forget, here were the twisted, yellow-bladed swords of a Mother-in-Law's Tongue. Presumably, whenever Jean thought of this hideous plant, she omitted the 'in-Law'. It was, he noticed, *Sansevieria trifasciata 'De fer'* – the new, super-rigid variety whose touch and texture almost lived up to its appearance.

Frank placed the money on the table beneath the striped blades of the *Sansevieria*: an offering on the altar of chagrin. Then he carried a plastic chair some way off and swung astride it so that she would be sure he couldn't easily make any sudden movements.

Without bothering to check the money, Jean perched on the edge of a small settee. And smiled again, smiting him more deeply than any of those sword blades could have done. Nearby stood a smaller table with some of her pottery craft gathering dust; she had given up on art.

'May I call you Jean? And please call me Frank.'

'Though that isn't your real name.'

'Oh, but it is. Frank by name, frank by – well, let's not mention Nature. I'll come straight to the point: we'd like to invite you to participate in an illegal DNA experiment – a highly illegal one, though it's one of which I'm sure you'll approve.'

She laughed.

'Illegal, by whose law? The genes are the only law, Frank. Look what their law has done to me.'

With her free hand she fumbled a cigarette from a packet; then hesitated.

'Go ahead, light it,' he reassured her. 'We aren't worried about you breaking any chromosomes by evil habits. We're way beyond all that sort of small change. I was, of course, referring to illegal in the public sense: the prohibition on playing roulette with the sacred image of God. Not that God doesn't play roulette with the universe, but apparently that's His business.'

'So you want an egg from me? Why, permission granted!' Jean exhaled smoke. 'No, that's crazy. I've heard of the goose that laid the golden egg – but worth a million? You must have some women on your team already. I hope you do!'

'Rest assured.'

'In that case, you must want me to play host mother . . . No, that's mad too. You could easily hire some poor cow for a tenth of that money – unless you're wanting her to give birth to a chimpanzee or a baby gorilla . . .'

'That's quite close, Jean. But you're looking in the wrong direction.'

'Let me guess.'

'You could guess till you're blue in the face. Besides, it's me who's paying for the guessing time. So listen: the Sponsor is a financial superman. But he wants to become an *actual* superman. He wants to become *Homo Superior* in his own life-time. He wants to sire supermen. Superwomen, too. He wants to give rise to the next race. And he'll be the first of them: the founder, Adam.

'Now, don't you grin! We aren't just playing a fool along for his money. Technically, it's all possible. *Now* it is. Though for obvious reasons we've kept quiet about it. Hence,' and Frank nodded in the direction of the plants, 'your generous retainer.'

'You're still taking a risk, telling me.'

'I think not. You're highly motivated, on *our* side of the fence. Besides which . . .'

'It's exactly the sort of thing I'd invent myself? To boost Jean Sandwich back into orbit? The mysterious visitor, the vast bribe, the anonymous super-rich Sponsor . . . Alas, you're so right! So: your Sponsor wants to be the new Adam, and I'm to be – ?'

'This time round, Eve will be created first. You see, we aren't absolutely positive we can pull it off with a human being. Though that's simply because we haven't tried, yet. The method definitely works with rats and chimps – which is why I said that you were quite close. The chimps are, well, superchimps now.'

'And what happened to the superrats?'

'We couldn't risk the superrats escaping into the wild. We had to destroy them. *Not*,' Frank hastened to add, 'that we have any intention of destroying the superchimps. That would be like killing your own cousin. And the Sponsor is a very scrupulous man.'

'Has he set up a trust fund for them, or something?'

'They enjoy delightful conditions. We did sterilize them, though, just as a precaution.'

'Yech.' Yet Jean accepted this. No doubt she was reflecting on the benefits which sterilization would have bestowed on her, had she been able to foresee the future.

'Merely vasectomies and ligatures, mind you. We didn't want to spoil their sex lives.'

Jean brightened. She set the gun aside, though it remained within easy reach.

'And how is this miracle of change accomplished?'

Frank mustered himself.

'I'm no expert, you understand, but briefly it depends on the fact that a great many gene sites are already "pre-adapted" for a sort of quantum leap to a new evolutionary level. Do you follow me? The old notion that evolution has to take hundreds of thousands of years has really gone out of the window. As we see it now, when change happens, it happens really quickly. It's like, well, a seed crystal suddenly altering the whole physical status of a saturated solution. Of course, it *might* take aeons before this does happen – before something triggers it. But the next evolutionary stage is sitting waiting in us all along. Like a butterfly in a chrysalis.'

'I know what was waiting in *me*.'

'That was just repetition.'

'It was a particularly unjust form of repetition!'

'It was just the same old record, with the stylus stuck in the groove. This is more like flipping the disc over to play what's on the other side. This isn't any of your ordinary tinkering with genes then recombining them. It's a question of nudging the whole works.'

'But *how*?'

'We've developed a self-replicating virus. It attaches to the DNA and spreads through all the cells in the body. That's the seed crystal. What is latent becomes actual, throughout the whole body. The flesh itself changes, not just the seed. The nerve networks form new connexions. The brain reorganizes itself. But the Sponsor wishes to behold the new being, Eve, before he commits himself to becoming Adam.'

'Do his scruples only extend to males, and chimps? Can't he find a man to volunteer?'

'You don't follow me. *He* has to be the first super-*man*. So only a woman can precede him. Only Eve.'

'I wonder whether that makes this a new, female cycle of creation? Or does it just make me a different sort of chimp?'

'Well, neither . . . though I take your point.'

Yet Jean's voice seemed full of zany anticipation. The feminist angle did not appear to bother her especially. As predicted. Her chagrin was aimed at something far deeper than simply sexist oppression.

'Actually,' Frank said coaxingly, 'we believe that the human potential for change is *huge*, compared with the rats and chimps. And they certainly did well enough.'

Jean grinned.

'Maybe I'll be able to fly through the air by will power? Maybe I'll become Wonder Woman?'

'Who knows?'

'I'll hardly need a million in the bank, then! Though,' she qualified quickly, 'it'll be handy to have it.'

'And have it you shall. But look, Jean: the money's more by way of reassurance – just in case the attempt doesn't succeed. If it does succeed, obviously you'll be the Sponsor's only peer on Earth. That implies a lot more than a million.'

'How do you mean, "in case"? Were there any mishaps with the chimps?'

'None whatever. What I meant was: in case nothing exciting happens. In case we have to go back to the drawing board.'

'I'd like to see these superchimps of yours before I make my mind up.'

'No problem. Be our guest. Come and spend a few days down on the Farm. That's what we call the Sponsor's spread in the country. Though it isn't a lot like an ordinary farm . . . It's more like Paradise – a real one. We can drive you down there right away, if you haven't anything else arranged. Not that I want to rush you.'

'I haven't. And you aren't.'

'It's about four hours' drive.'

'Good. I'd enjoy a drive in the country. I haven't seen any real landscape for ages.'

'Ah, I'll have to disappoint you there. We have curtains in the back of the Merc. I trust you won't mind if they're closed? You'll appreciate the need for discretion.'

'So I'll bring my Travel Scrabble. Do you play Scrabble?'

'Yes. But I cheat. I make very long words by adding extra syllables. My own house rule is that if you can think up a single plausible sentence using a word, then it's kosher. For example:

we're going to unsandwich you, Jean. We're going to regenerate you, unsandwichingly.'

Jean's laughter was a shower of silver.

'If I say yes, to the unsandwiching.'

'I'm fairly sure you will. You might even say we're banking on it.'

Before they left apartment 804, Jean took care to water all the house plants. With one exception. She left the Mother-in-Law's Tongue bone dry. Yet such neglect would have little effect. A *Sansevieria* was a plant without sensibility. Like mother Josie, like daughter Alison.

Chapter 4

To Frank's eyes, the Farm was indeed a Garden of Eden. The Sponsor was generally an absent God, who only paid flying visits there by helicopter. He spent the bulk of his time up in his penthouse heaven on top of King Enterprises Building.

But obviously Bruno King would shift the centre of his power from the skyscraper to the Farm, when he altered his role from that of God, to Adam. Frank regarded this prospect with a certain mild jealousy, for up until now the Farm had been his own to roam as he pleased. Child of the city, it had delighted him in his free time to wander its wilder domains all alone.

Sealed up as tightly as an air base, though with far less public visibility, the Farm (once you left the complex of buildings in the northernmost sector) was a wild garden of woods and lakes and hills.

Oaks and pines and maples grew there; and apple and cherry orchards. Wild strawberries spread on heathy upland, near unraided beehives. Irises and bullrushes choked a marsh. Slabby rocks were jungled over with azaleas and rhododendrons. Streams ran through stands of old forest into an unfished river stocked with trout and perch and chub. Muntjac deer scampered for cover at dawn and dusk. Pheasant whirred aloft, safe from any hunter's bullet, while mallard, coot and water-hens nested round the reedy lakes. And funeral cypresses marched in rows, reminding Frank of a certain cemetery which had been his closest contact with Nature when he was a city boy.

Stone and marble buildings were scattered about the estate, too, in the unlikeliest places: pavilions, temples, arches, a turreted folly, a rotondo, and a monumental column resembling an inland lighthouse. The wanderer generally came upon these by surprise. Pebbled grottoes were cut into rock-sides, mouths adrip with ferns and mosses; while rivulets spilling down the hillsides were cunningly routed through the bubbling lips of stone grotesques.

Closer to the Farm complex proper, were formal lawns and a complicated yew-hedge maze.

The estate spread over twelve square miles, and a belt of dense forest shrouded the whole perimeter, with an electrified double fence striding through it.

As soon as Craig McKinnon reported from the front of the limousine by intercom that they had passed through the main gate, Frank opened all the curtains.

Jean and he had played four games of Scrabble, and Jean had won three of them. They had also shared a picnic lunch, washing pâté and smoked salmon sandwiches down with chilled Hock from the small refrigerator.

Now bars of sunlight flashed epileptically as Reuben Maccoby piloted the Mercedes along a forest road. Rounding a final bend, they emerged into the open.

Guernsey cows grazed a meadow beyond a horse paddock. To their right, the Farm buildings followed the inner edge of the forest barrier for a thousand yards. To their left extended the inner fence which enclosed Eden. Its own gate still stood wide open in the distance, though really Frank was the only dedicated wanderer. The other employees generally stuck close to the amusements and sports facilities.

Several slim windmills spun their sails, and an artesian well tapped the water table. A flagpole rose outside the ranch house, though no flag was run up the tack line; as usual the Sponsor was not in residence. Frank pointed out the staff village, the games centre, the helipad, the milking sheds, the security tower, the solar panels on the roof of the ranch house . . . and the science area, adjacent to the walled Superchimp compound.

'Superchimps first.' Frank rapped on the glass and gestured.

Maccoby had to detour on to the lawn to avoid a family of geese out for a walk.

An armed guard sat ensconced on top of the high stone wall, in a glass cabin. At his command a steel door rolled back to admit the Mercedes into a long, stout cage, then he locked them in for scrutiny. Satisfied, the guard operated the inner mesh-gate and lowered a drawbridge beyond.

A broad moat lapped the inside circuit of the wall. Alligators were basking on the bank. A barbed wire fence, decorated with red lightning flash signs, kept those snappy creatures by the water.

'But it's like a prison camp!'

In vain did Jean search the barren compound for any sign of gambolling chimps. A blank concrete building, in the shape of a horseshoe, hunched around the north lip of a deep crater or pit; that was all.

'The shock you'd get from the fence isn't lethal,' Frank explained genially. 'And the alligators are strictly a fun thing. It's *water* that Pongo loathes.'

Jean withdrew into her seat.

'You said they had delightful quarters!' she accused.

'Oh, they *do*. Pongo never sees up here. We sincerely hope pongo never will.'

The Mercedes halted outside the windowless building. Frank hopped out and ran round to open Jean's door, to escort her to the steel-clad entrance. He spoke into an intercom.

'Frank Caldero, accompanying our special guest. Peter Piper picked a peck of pickled peppers.

'Pongo can't imitate the human voice,' he commented. 'Their air pipes are too short. They haven't got vocal cords in their necks.'

'But this is ridiculous! I don't care how super they are – Harry Houdini himself couldn't get out of here. Is this the fine and private place?'

'No, no, and no. You'll be perfectly free to roam.'

Did Jean detect a note of envy in his voice?

'Look: ordinary chimps are damn clever. Leave them a length of bamboo, and they'll invent the vaulting pole. Superchimps are an unknown quantity. They're *aliens*, essentially. Alien intelligences.'

'So don't they have any rights?'

'Does anyone? Beyond the right to starve, and fall sick, and get mugged, and be miserable? Our superchimps enjoy the *privilege* of a happy life. But we must safeguard it. I don't *say* that they have any secret plans up their furry sleeves. But they're all curiosity with a capital C. And if one of them got out, we'd all be in very hot water.'

'So this is all for their sake.'

'Right.'

'But you said all sorts of physical alterations happen: evolutionary changes. Why haven't they grown vocal cords and longer windpipes?'

As Jean was asking the question, the steel door was opened by a red-headed woman wearing outsize jeans and an open lab coat. Underneath was a white zipped-up plastic windcheater. Her mountainous bust looked as though it was bound with a huge bandage. She beamed.

'I'm Robina. Robina Weber. And you're the volunteer! Welcome, welcome. Naturally, you've come to see how our metapongids are getting on – and the answer's *famously*.'

Jean resisted an urge to glance back at the barbed wire, moat and alligators.

'Oh, not as famously as *that*! Nobody outside knows a thing.'

Robina chuckled.

'Caught you out there! Working with the metapongids, a person gets hyped up on all kinds of body language. You *almost* looked at the moat.'

'Metapongids equals superchimps,' explained Frank.

'You don't say.'

'I can answer that question of yours about their speech equipment. But come on in first – we mustn't leave doors standing open.'

Robina drew back with a rush which pulled Jean and Frank inside the building, virtually by suction. Linking arms with Jean, Robina hauled her along a corridor then down a long flight of steps, patting her comfortingly all the while. At the bottom, Robina finally released Jean.

'Do excuse me! Just my grooming reflexes at work!'

The room they now entered harboured video screens and racks of tape spools. The far wall was glass from floor to ceiling. From this observation window, the spectator looked down into the 'crater'. Roofed with clear perspex, the hole in the ground bellied out into a great, bright cave floored with soil and illuminated by mirrors bouncing sunlight from above. The cave was a planthouse of hibiscus, passion flower vines, bamboo groves, banana trees, palms, lianas. One section was devoted to gymnastic equipment. There were two huts elsewhere, roofed with plastic thatch, and a pair of open booths equipped with TV sets. In one of these booths sat a pair of superchimps at their ease, their fingers fluttering as they watched a film.

Another superchimp was working out on the parallel bars. The fourth, and closest, was ambling through the bamboo grove below, scratching itself. The superchimp walked erect, though in a bow-legged way. Its face was a buckled grey mask with squashed, flaring nostrils and a floppy-lipped muzzle, surrounded by a mane of black hair rather like some nineteenth-century Russian novelist's. Cauliflower ears stuck out to the sides.

Unlike a Russian novelist, though, luxurious hair covered all the rest of its body too, apart from the fingers and the feet. The superchimp's forehead receded less than that of any chimp that Jean recalled seeing on trips to the zoo, when Alison was little. Its eyes were black and bright. It stood almost five feet tall.

Noticing the observers, it waved a long arm to them, then made signs. After waving back exuberantly with both arms, Robina signed in reply.

'What's he saying?' asked Jean.

'No, he doesn't "say". He signs. That isn't the same thing as "saying". To answer your earlier question: metapongids don't sprout vocal cords because they aren't inclined that way. In the wild, a pongo doesn't react to an alarm call by answering it – but with action.'

'If somebody screams "Fire!" I'm going to get the hell out, not stand around asking questions.'

'But this has deeper implications. Theirs is a semantics of action, you see, not abstraction. *We* may believe that we're teaching them abstract thought – merely because we can evoke a response that seems appropriate. But *they're* just playing a drama-game with us – and the name of the game in this case is Abstract Thought. They play it bloody well, incidentally. It's like, well, trying to carry on a conversation about evolution with a dyed-in-the-wool God Nut. You're both talking the same language, *but*. So just remember this: the metapongids aren't ever thinking what *you* think they're thinking. They grasp the world. They don't hold it at arms' length like we do.'

'It doesn't seem to me they've *got* a vast amount of world.'

'There's plenty, Jean. Besides, they watch a lot of TV and movies. It's no worse than having to spend your life on board a starship.'

'Not that anybody's ever tried.'

'A starship without a destination,' added Frank helpfully. 'Their ship isn't going anywhere. But where are any of us going in the long run? Well, that's what the Sponsor means to find out. In practice, not in the abstract.'

'Can they, um, compare "before" with "now"? Can they explain what it means *to them* to have become superchimps?'

'They don't "explain". They exemplify it. But let's not get bogged down in metapongid psychology. That's my business. Fascinating as it is, it's a side-track from the main concern.'

'But are they *happy*?'

'Let's go down. Ask them yourself. I'll interpret. But remember,' and Robina twitched her hands, 'whatever I translate into words has a very different *feel* to it when I sign it. It's more like ballet, then. And ballet doesn't say; it shows. Another thing: the new sign combinations they've invented on their own in no way match our own words and phrases one-to-one. My hands dance the ballet with them, but increasingly *they're* taking over the choreography.'

'You mean you don't know what they're saying to each other all the time?'

'Depends. They're fluent in Amerslan. But that's only a basis.'

'So even with all that video gear you don't know what they're discussing? What they're . . . planning?'

'There's no malice in superpongo,' said Frank reassuringly. 'He's a really friendly fellow.'

'But not offensively so,' added Robina. 'When they meet a newcomer, which is obviously seldom, well, they understand *all* about defensible body distance. They can read us in ways we can't read each other. Though I *am* beginning to catch on. They're, well they're just simply super – in more ways than one.'

'Ah, but would you let your daughter marry one?'

'Aha. In your case,' began Frank . . .

'In my case it would classify as cruelty to pongos. And don't I know it! Should my daughter ever notice the difference.'

Gazing down at the superchimps, Jean felt sad. They too had been hauled up by their bootstraps. Then the bootstraps had been tied in knots. Ligatures and vasectomies.

Chapter 5

Robina thrust the armoured glass door open as soon as the green light came on, and they walked out into the subterranean garden.

Jasmine fragrance assaulted Jean. And Robina was assaulted too, by the superchimp. But gently so. He draped an arm over her. With horny fingernails he tickled her scalp, while his right hand flashed quick signs. It seemed to Jean that the superchimp was reacting to Robina the way a human being treats a pet, rather than the other way about.

But it was the human beings who had sterilized the superchimps . . . *Did the superchimps know that?* Could they smell the difference in themselves, while they still remained sexually active? Doubtless they were aware that no superchimp babies had been born, or were on the way. Or were they any wiser about the origin of babies than South Sea Islanders had once been?

'Caesar wishes to know who you are, Jean. What kind of person. How you relate to Frank and me. What things delight you.'

'Plants delight me. And I play Scrabble.'

Robina fluttered signs.

'I skipped the Scrabble. So now you're a gardener. Let Caesar touch you. Let him read your emotions in your muscle tone.'

Jean held out her hand. Caesar took it. Turning it over, he scrutinized her palm like a fortune teller. His own hand felt rough, warm and hard. He let go of her, stroked her cheek briefly with his knuckles; and that sufficed.

He signed; Robina verbalized.

'Will you be gardening down here?'

Jean shook her head.

'Alas,' mimed Caesar.

'Might I ask a few questions of my own?'

The other three superchimps had now arrived. Caesar signed busily, to up-date them.

'Sure, but keep them reasonable. The questions. The names of the other three are Cleopatra, Brutus and Boadicaea.'

Jean addressed Caesar; immediately he looked to Robina's hands.

'When you say "down here", Caesar, what do you suppose goes on "up there"?'

Frank whistled softly. But Robina's hands flashed, unperturbed. The reply came back:

'If I'm considering "down here", I'm not considering "up there", am I?'

'Yes, but what do you suppose happens up there – outside?'

'"Down here" is *our* world,' interpreted Robina. '"Up there" is the other world. That's the place where they make the movies. It's a dangerous, smelly world.'

'True enough!'

'We go there when we die,' volunteered Caesar. Frank darted a quick glance at Robina. She frowned at him; then frowned at herself for having frowned.

'That's a new one,' murmured Frank in a deliberately flat tone.

Robina signed of her own accord, questioning Caesar. Presently she explained:

'That wasn't a religious statement. It was purely practical. Pragmatic. Waste goes up: dead flowers, excrement, fallen leaves. Dead bodies are waste. QED.'

'So we live in the shit up there?' mused Jean. 'Don't I know it.'

All four superchimps were watching the humans closely, fascinated by the brief flurry which Caesar's impromptu remark had caused. Had Caesar *intended* this? Once more, Jean suspected that the tables were somehow being turned.

He's capable of making a monkey of us, she thought. She noticed Brutus signing behind his back at Boadicaea. Or was he merely scratching himself?

'Why *do* people make movies up there?' she asked him.

'Movies are not made,' translated Robina dutifully. 'Movies are real. Only cartoons are made. And those,' and now while she spoke Caesar mimed sleep, with his eyes aflutter from rapid eye movements, 'those are your dreams.'

'Good God,' said Frank. 'Caesar thinks we dream about weirdo animals. Disney rules Slumberland. He films our dreams.'

'Wasn't that Disney's whole idea?' asked Jean innocently.

'Idiot. He's making a distinction between realism and fantasy. And *that's* pretty interesting.'

'Really? I don't know what movies you *do* show them – movies as opposed to cartoons – but I'd hardly say movies are always very realistic. I mean, take *King Kong* or *Superman*, to name but two. Incidentally, *have* they – ?'

'Of course! We don't show them junk. Those are two of their favourite films. Jack Nimmo, who's off duty right now, he interprets the sound tracks for them into gestures, first time round – but for repeats, they never bother with hand-dubbing. Actually, Jack suspects they're all pretty sharp at following speech. But I doubt it. He says they don't let on. It preserves their, hmm . . . Gives them time to think – like the Soviet Foreign Minister. He can speak English, but he uses his interpreters as a delaying tactic. Well, that's Jack's theory.'

'Isn't it a bit provocative, showing them *King Kong*?'

Frank chuckled.

'Shows them what'll happen if they try to escape.'

'And they love *The Sound of Music*.'

'I don't get it. Those are all escapist movies. What's so dangerous and smelly about them? Well, maybe from their point of view *King Kong* . . .'

Robina signed, and Caesar traced a swastika in the air, and made other signs.

'Smelly Nazis in *The Sound of Music*. Bang-bang hoodlums in *Superman*. It's a smelly world, says Caesar.'

The superchimp raised both arms above his head, and made as if to leap and fly into the air. He pointed enquiringly at Frank.

Frank laughed, and shook his head.

'Only in airplanes, old buddy. Perceptive of you, though.'

Cleopatra ambled forward. What she now proceeded to act out was, to Jean's eyes, a truly amazing mime; and the meaning of it could only be this: 'As *we* are, compared with what we were before; so are you people now – *to what exactly*?' But then Cleopatra went on to sketch elephant ears looping up around her own ears – ah no, they were Mickey Mouse ears! The superchimp pulled her lips into a beak, like Donald Duck's, and quacked. She ended by scratching her skull and banging her brow in puzzlement.

'So if we aren't going to change into Superman,' thought Jean, perplexed, 'that only leaves the cartoon characters of our dreams . . . to model ourselves on? Does it?'

Apparently the superchimps were well aware that the humans intended to change themselves . . . What else did they know about it?

'I didn't catch all that,' confessed Robina.

'I think I did,' Jean said quietly.

'Well, she was telling you her favourite cartoons.'

'No, more than that.'

Cleopatra stepped up to Jean and patted her, cooing softly. And Jean heard in her coo of approval that Cleopatra *understood*. She knew the change that had happened to herself. She suspected that Jean was to be the next candidate. And she wasn't warning Jean; she was encouraging her.

Then and there, Jean made up her mind.

'You can count me in,' she said to Frank. 'I accept. How soon do we get started?'

'Oh . . . in, well, in about three days' time . . . we can start, yes. We'll want to run some medical tests first. We need to get you measured up. Test your eyesight and stamina and IQ and so on. For comparison. There's the financial business, too. I'd say, about four days. I must say I'm *delighted* to hear – '

'Fine. Let's get on with it.'

'Well, yes. I suppose you'll want to go back to your apartment first to sort things out?'

'You mean, arrange my disappearance properly? No, Frank, I never want to see that place again. Ah, my plants though: I oughtn't to abandon them . . .'

'I'll bring them down to the Farm. I'll see to it personally.'

With a brightly conspiratorial glance at Jean, Cleopatra ran to a nearby banana plant. Snapping off a yellow fruit, she scaled a vine-clad pergola.

'Do so, Frank. I'm sure you can look after everything just fine. Do so.'

Chuckling deep in her throat, the superchimp tossed the skin down accurately at Jean's feet.

Had it not been for this interruption, Jean might well have remembered to add, 'But *don't* bother about the *Sansevieria*. It can become an *Egyptian* mummy – in the tomb of my room!' And she might also have laughed joyously and recklessly.

As it was, she had to avoid treading on the banana skin as she made her way back towards the armoured glass door and elevator.

Chapter 6

Four days later to the hour, Jean let her robe drop and lay down naked on a huge white bed.

Frank admired Jean's body unrestrainedly, since his expression was conveniently hidden by the surgical mask insisted on by Dr Ohira, and he wore a tent of a lab coat. His eyes saluted her breasts. Yet he knew that this was in likely farewell to the woman she had been until today.

Did the Sponsor – who was watching remotely from his penthouse – admire Jean and desire her too, as she was at present? Frank doubted this. To Jean, the present perfection of the flesh only hid a deeper imperfection. To Bruno King, it merely masked his dream.

The bed was of flexible foam, able to conform to any bodily alterations. Not that any really drastic ones were expected. Jean wasn't, for instance, likely to sprout wings. The bed also incorporated stress gauges to record any weight loss or weight gain. Catheters and intravenous drips and vital sign monitors lay in a spaghetti tangle, waiting to be connected.

Frank visualized the bed as a great slab of white bread. Upon it, Jean lay sandwiched between the past of the human race, and the future. But the future was invisible as yet. Thus she was an open sandwich.

Dr Shiba hovered near her with the hypodermic which would send her to sleep. Once she was unconscious, Shiba would connect up all the plumbing. Then, at the Godly word of command from the Sponsor, Ohira would inject the virus itself.

Based on the chimp precedent, the virus ought to take a day to establish itself in her body and a couple more days to spread through every cell, then five days more to express itself in a new Jean: the Super-Eve.

Were she awake, the final days would be painful ones, for her flesh would be reabsorbing itself and generating new tissue, while her nervous system rewired itself. So she would not be revived till the process had run its full course. She would spend the whole period of her change, comatose – as had the chimps before her, and the second batch of rats. The first trial run with rats had been cut short on Bruno King's command when the rats showed signs of extreme distress. Whether the rats had actually been in extreme pain was another matter; but the Sponsor had no wish to torture any living creature.

While Jean remained in isolation, her waste products would be pumped away into a holding tank, and the plastic sausages of vitamin-enriched glucose which nourished her would be topped up automatically.

'Good luck,' said Shiba. He slipped the first needle into Jean's arm.

She winked at him.

'*Banzai!* Here's one in the eye for Mother Nature! But it isn't . . . question of luck . . . is it? Where's . . . Frank?'

Frank redirected his gaze from Jean's nipples, to her eyes.

'Right here.'

'Luck's random. This isn't . . . random. This is . . . is . . . .'

Jean did not say what this was; for she was already asleep.

The next fifteen minutes passed in connecting Jean up, and checking the connections. Then Shiba spoke to Ohira in Japanese.

'*Ima, sensei!*'

Ohira unlocked the refrigerator. From a crowded rack inside he took a small bottle. Squeezing a hypodermic through the cap, he sucked up all the contents.

'We are ready now, Mr Caldero.'

Frank unclipped the flat orange scrambler phone from inside his jacket. Politely he addressed the video camera.

'Ready to proceed on your word, sir.'

The voice which came from the button in his ear was bird-like: twangy, sing-song, high-pitched with excitement – even though King had not spoken up until now. King might be excited, yet he wasn't jittery. This, after all, was Eve not Adam. But now the Sponsor could not resist making a little speech. For Frank's ears only? No, it would be recorded for posterity in the KE computer.

'This moment is the fulcrum, Frank. It's the turning point of all future time. Here is the first lungfish crawling on to land. Here is the first bird taking off. Here is the capture of fire. All of these, rolled into one! Well, let's hope so . . . So I say unto you: *Go Ahead*.'

Frank nodded to Ohira, and the doctor promptly injected Jean.

Inevitably, the hypodermic needle reminded Frank of God's creative finger up on the Sistine Chapel roof.

But then, Frank always was a sucker for the obvious. Such as Jean's nipples, for instance. Regretfully, he removed himself from their vicinity. The die was cast; the evolutionary Rubicon was being forded.

Chapter 7

The transformation of Jean into Jean-Eve began three days after the injection. Day by day, the alterations became ever more grossly obvious to Frank and the other onlookers.

Her face grew plumper, with an expression which was a weird blend of cunning and vacuity. Ohira surmised that this was simply due to retensioning of the facial muscles, coupled with the soporific drug.

She put on fat all over, draining the supply of fortified glucose far faster than anticipated; the reservoir itself had to be topped up. Her chin was engulfed, and doubled. Her neat breasts swelled. Her creamy skin grew ruddy, as though exposed to a cold wind for many weeks; at the same time her temperature soared, from the fever of the change in her. Her pageboy hair all fell out, then grew back at amazing speed, thick and black and greasy, as though her scalp had become a spinning loom. Her skeletal structure enlarged; she became not merely fat, but more massive.

Frank watched through the observation window from day to day, bemused, wondering how Bruno King was reacting to this metamorphosis as he too looked in on it, from afar. The person evolving on the white bed did possess a sort of coarse Rubens magnificence, yet she was hardly a beauty queen by any contemporary standard. Yet the Sponsor did not complain. Indeed, he made no comment at all.

Of one thing Frank was already sure: this new person certainly wasn't Jean's mother, reborn in Jean's flesh. Nor was it anything remotely like daughter Alison, as extrapolated into adulthood.

The chimp precedent proved misleading, as regards the time scale. By the seventh day of the metamorphosis much of Jean's new fat had compacted into well-buffered muscle, and she was a prima donna Wagnerian Valkyrie with huge bosoms and limbs. She had become a giantess two metres tall and proportionately girthed, massing almost two hundred kilos. By now the Rubens-like impression had yielded to something out of heroic legend. She was one of the giants who predated the Gods on Earth. She was the first type of being to emerge from out of the icy void: a troll woman, who could easily have snatched Thor's hammer away from him with one hand.

By the tenth day she was two and a quarter metres tall (or long) and she massed well over two hundred kilos.

Was this to be the future of the human race? wondered Frank. A race of giants? The old myth of the descent of human beings from the giants of earlier days was being reversed before his very eyes.

Yet was this giantess clever – or was she dumb? Had all that nutrition been poured into mere bone and tissue? What had become of Jean's sharp mind?

By the twelfth day the changes seemed to have stopped. Shiba halted the soporific sedative and disconnected Jean from the drips and catheters. She slept on, naturally.

On the next day, early in the morning, she awoke.

Waiting in the changing room were the two Japanese gene-doctors and Frank. Playing cards in the observation room next door were McKinnon and Maccoby: two muscular orderlies. Watching from his penthouse suite several hundred miles away, paged by Frank at dawn, was the Sponsor.

'She's conscious,' announced Ohira.

Jean had opened her eyes.

'Now, sir,' said Frank into the scrambler phone.

The giantess lay still for a while, as though trying to remember who she was, yet not quite succeeding because now she was Jean transformed.

Suddenly a joyful grin spread over her great face. She arose in a single motion, her mighty muscles rippling: a female Samson or Goliath with thongs of oily hair whipping her shoulders.

Stepping away from the white foam bed, she gazed at herself in a long mirror. And laughed boomingly, slapping her palms against her thighs with all the exuberance of a proud gorilla.

'How do you feel?' ventured Ohira. He and Shiba were a couple of shaved monkeys in white coats; and Frank felt no sturdier than a chipmunk.

Jean grinned hugely.

'I feel like a million dollars. *And* I feel like swallowing my daughter for breakfast. Or perhaps a roast ox. Feed me!' she ordered. She glanced about the aseptic room, as though this was actually some cave littered with carcasses and bones.

The two doctors and Frank were now competing in offering her chairs, but she dismissed the seating as far too miniature. Marching to the negative-pressure airlock, she tossed first one steel door jarringly open, then the second, disrupting the airlock mechanism and setting off an alarm bell. Striding into the observation room, she thumped herself on to the steel table there, scattering the two orderlies and their card game. McKinnon retreated to bar the outer door with his body. Maccoby shut the alarm off, then joined him. They stood together with arms folded: two nervous wrestlers hoping to avoid a bout.

Collecting the largest smock available, Frank hastened after the giantess. She accepted the garment with an ironic nod, and pulled it over her head, the better to demonstrate its inadequacy. The smock parted at the seams. She balled the torn fabric up, blew her nose boisterously to clear her sinuses and tossed the used rag aside.

'I shall wear robes,' she announced. 'Something long and strong and bright, with a leather belt, and thong sandals.'

'It'll take a while.'

She waved Frank's apology aside with a great hand. The draught was terrific.

'Maccoby, you heard the lady. Go and see to it.' It was fairly obvious that the two 'orderlies' were quite outclassed, in any case. Looking relieved, Maccoby hurried from the room.

'You *are* still . . . Jean?' Frank framed the question cautiously.

'I have eaten Jean,' proclaimed the giantess. 'Jean is too mean a name for me. She was just *hors d'oeuvres*. But I'm the main course. I shall call myself . . . well, I'll decide that after breakfast.'

'McKinnon, the lady needs feeding.'

Presently, sitting vastly naked on the table, Jean-that-was demolished five steaks in a row, and a dozen fried eggs, washed down with half a gallon of milk. Frank was beginning to wonder – as, no doubt, were Ohira and Shiba – where exactly to draw the line between exuberance and madness.

After her mega-breakfast, the giantess belched appreciatively.

'This room's too small,' she remarked. 'All your rooms are puny. I need great halls.' She waved at the camera which scanned the observation room. 'Hi there, Sponsor! When are the next Olympic Games?'

Frank's spirits were in his shoes now, and maybe the two Japanese were wondering whether to disembowel themselves. Surely Bruno King couldn't contemplate congress with this titan? And he was certainly no sports promoter – even if 'Jean' did now seem like the ultimate East German athlete, pumped up with anabolic steroids.

Yet on the other hand, thought Frank with a grain of hope, maybe she *was* on to something, if she was as fleet of foot as she was mighty . . .

That wasn't the point, damn it! The whole point of the exercise was to find out what a future superbeing would be like. If they were all like this, the human race (*Superior* variety) would quickly eat itself into extinction.

And come to think of it, maybe that was what really went wrong for the dinosaurs. They had dined too sumptuously. They had cleaned the board, and left nothing for the next meal.

'I know! I shall call myself *Geneva*. That's Jean – plus Eva, from

35

Eve. And all my money's in the bank in Switzerland.' She laughed, deafening Frank.

The Sponsor whispered in Frank's ear.

'Could you say that again, sir? It's kind of noisy in here.'

'I said: she isn't exactly what I expected. But then, none of us knew what to expect, did we? I am . . . shocked – and pleased, too. Such strength and presence warms my heart, Frank. I can hardly feel amorously attracted to her, but naturally I'm still viewing her with the eyes of Now, not with the eyes of one transformed. Could a pre-human hominid feel sexually attracted by a specimen of *Homo Sapiens*? Hardly! I *do* recognize this, Frank. Perhaps you thought that I expected a Primavera or an Aphrodite? Rather than a titan? *Not necessarily*. You've done remarkable work. Please tell Ohira and Shiba that I'm pleased with them. At the moment I can't *like* her. Yet there is admiration in my soul for the prodigy she is.

'I'm coming down in person, Frank. Anybody in the world may be ordinarily handsome or clever or strong. But we seek the extraordinary, don't we? I certainly do. I'll need a few days to re-arrange my affairs at this end. I don't think I'm going to be very interested in my old life-style in a few weeks' time, but of course one must keep hold of the reins. I too shall be a prodigy. We two will be the first of a new race.'

'What about Jean? I mean Geneva.'

'Request her to stick around, till we can meet on equal terms. That's part of her contract. Meanwhile, tell Maccoby to redouble the security precautions.'

'Will do.'

As soon as Frank had clipped the phone inside his jacket again, he told the two doctors of the Sponsor's pleasure. Immediately the Japanese abandoned all restraint. For a whole minute and more they clapped each other and Frank on the back. Luckily Geneva refrained from joining in. Indeed, she wore a quizzical expression on her face.

'I'd forgotten about *him*,' she said.

'He's part of the deal,' Frank reminded her, gingerly.

'Ho, ho. He'll need to be superb, to bowl me over.'

Frank couldn't visualize the Sponsor, or anybody else, bowling Geneva over and taking her in rut. Personally he would prefer a few inches of sheet steel between himself and any tryst of the titans.

'Point taken. He'll need to be.'

Of course, McKinnon or Maccoby could always shoot a hypodermic dart into Geneva – primed with something suitable for stunning a rhino, say – whereupon Ohira could perform the task of conception by artificial insemination . . . Yet Frank doubted that the Sponsor had any such sleight of sperm in mind. Bruno King had sounded quite intoxicated by the coming wedding of the giants.

Chapter 8

Duly robed and thong-sandalled, Geneva spent the following days sprinting about the estate. She splashed through lakes. She scaled hills. She crashed through thickets. Her amazing new body seemed quite tireless.

McKinnon and Maccoby did their best to keep track of her; and Frank was relieved to learn that Geneva made no attempts on the electrified frontier fence. Yet why should she? She wasn't particularly in prison, and if she took it into her head to burst out, barrelling straight through the main gate, where could she ever find a sufficiently plentiful supply of steaks and such in the rural vicinity? Raw, on the hoof? Doubtless the idea of roaming the countryside like some Grecian-attired Bigfoot possessed little appeal.

Six days after Geneva's forceful exit from the changing room, Frank sat at the wheel of the Mercedes as Bruno King's helicopter, with its bold silver coronet motif painted on the side, came down to land on the helipad.

He waited till the rotor blades had stopped turning before he hopped out and opened the rear door of the limousine. McKinnon would be most annoyed if the inside got filled with dust.

Bruno King descended from the helicopter. He was a weedy specimen of a man. Or perhaps a wiry one, depending on one's point of view. Whenever Frank saw him, before King's personality overwhelmed him, he couldn't help but think at first (being a sucker for the obvious) of those classic advertisements for body-building regimens, where the beach boy kicks sand in the face of the runt. King had obviously developed his financial muscle to bursting point, but when it came to making his body superhuman only science was going to help him, not work-outs.

Actually, Bruno King had some trouble with his digestion, as a result of which he subsisted on a diet of malted milk, oysters, soft-boiled eggs, honey and vitamins; which, perhaps, was why he had trouble with his digestion.

The Sponsor's face was birdlike, with a beak of a nose and brown beady eyes. Today he wore a deerstalker with a jaunty green feather stuck in it, and a red-checked lumber jacket zipped up to his chin, as if it was his intention to hunt Geneva through the woods of his estate. With approval he noted that the flag was run up the pole (with a fluttering coronet on it).

'Where is she, Frank?'

'Out roaming, sir.'

'I suppose I couldn't expect her to mount an honour guard. Where's Maccoby?'

'Out keeping tabs.'

King glanced sceptically at the waiting limousine, as though it had been parked deliberately so as to get in his way. His eyes charted a tentative course around the long Mercedes. Rejecting this option, he climbed into the back of the limousine, shuffled across to the far side and opened the other door. His intended route led *directly* from helicopter to changing room, and he did not intend to deviate an inch from it. Climbing out, he set off on foot for the medical centre.

Frank had already shut the passenger door politely behind King and was back in the driver's seat, with the engine on, before he noticed. Hastily abandoning the Mercedes, he rushed after his master.

'I *can* drive, you know!' he protested.

'Sure you can. You always drive that thing like a hearse when I'm in it. I like some pizazz in my drivers. Anyway, while we're walking over I want to outline the attorney situation. The whole show is set up to run like clockwork from the KE Building, theoretically for ever more. But you, Frank, will possess right of attorney to change corporate basics on my say-so from here.'

'But you can't trust an employee with something like that! I might be a boring driver, but – '

'*With certain qualifications*, Frank. There are code-words for each possible event. You'll receive them from me, and pass them on. That's if I can't be bothered to pick up a phone to call KEB myself. Or physically *can't* pick up a phone. And here,' and King burrowed in his lumber jacket, 'are sealed instructions for various wild card events.'

Frank leafed through the packet. The enclosed envelopes were labelled: '*In the Event of Death*', '*In the Event of Brain Death*', '*In the Event of Homicidal Insanity*' . . .

'From here on in, I wish to define what constitutes "sane" behaviour on my part. In the envelope headed "*In the Event of Apparent Insanity*" you'll find a special sanity test I've had drawn up, with precisely this in mind. You'll appreciate that sanity for me isn't necessarily the same thing as sanity for the next fellow.'

Frank nodded brightly. He glanced back at the Mercedes, forlornly unattended with two doors wide open and the breeze blowing through. He noticed faint fumes puffing from the exhaust pipe.

'I'm depositing duplicates of this package with Ohira and Maccoby.'

'Christ, sir, I wouldn't give Maccoby – !'

'Reuben owes me deep loyalty, Frank. So deep, it's almost embarrassing what he'd do for me.'

Frank swallowed.

'Well, so long as you're – '

'Oh, I am. I've deposited a further copy with John Schaeffer at KEB. So it's all tied up, and it's knotted tight into the silicon guts of the KEB computer.'

'I just realized, I left the engine running,' said Frank in anguish.

'Sort that out later. Right now, I wish to get changed.'

'But it might start off on its own.'

'Leave it. Life's too short, Frank.'

Frank noticed that Craig McKinnon was sprinting along past the maze, heading towards the limousine. Reaching the Mercedes, he leapt in and gunned the engine, bringing the vehicle round with a howl of tyres in a neat manoeuvre which successfully slammed the passenger door shut *en route*, before skidding to a halt outside the medical centre.

'More like that,' said King softly. 'You see?' He walked on in.

'You couldn't park a poodle,' sneered McKinnon, as he caught up with Frank and shoved him inside. 'Why don't you get your eyes tested *again*?'

'*Shazam*,' swore Frank forlornly. 'Oh, *shazam* it!'

'Don't you blaspheme at me in Hindu.'

'In Hindi. The language is called Hindi. Anyway, that wasn't Hindi.'

'I know what it was. Captain Marvel. I read comics too.'

'Do you read anything else?'

Frank felt the flat pressure of McKinnon's holstered pistol up against his spine. He walked faster.

'More respect for the King's attorney, please,' he called over his shoulder.

McKinnon sniggered.

Chapter 9

Now that he was stripped off, Bruno King may have reminded the two Japanese of an *origami* figure: he was a man made of tightly-folded, pinkish-white paper. Ohira and Shiba, of course, were far more interested in what he would look like when he was *un*folded . . .

King was duly put to sleep on the white bed; he was connected up and injected.

Three days later, while Geneva continued to thrash ebulliently around the estate, the changes began.

Like Jean, King proceeded to go through what Frank now thought of as the stage of banal caricature. Yet whereas Geneva had seemed for a while merely fat, stupid and sly, during the corresponding period of his change Bruno King actually shrank, becoming very reminiscent of an Egyptian mummy; he dried up and shrivelled. It seemed that not only were the catheters draining fluid from his body, but that the feeding tubes were emptying him too. He was regressing into some wizened, primitive monkey-man.

Frank viewed this with concern – as did the two bodyguards, for they were watching the body they were paid to guard evaporate before their very eyes. McKinnon and Maccoby had worked out a rota between them so that one or the other would always be in the observation room, playing solitaire or studying comic books. From here on, Geneva had to be left to her own devices.

Then, King stabilized.

Yet he did not build back. Instead – weighing by now less than fifteen kilos, and measuring just a metre long from head to foot – he became something ineffably beautiful: a sprite, an elfin creature, fairy-like, angelic.

Frank was consumed with wonder, mingled with anxiety.

Ohira took him aside one day, out of hearing of McKinnon.

'This *can't* be the future of the human race, Mr Caldero. Giant ladies, and tiny males! It wouldn't work, not with our species. We aren't spiders! I believe that what's really happening is a peculiar kind of *psychobiological* change. The subject becomes what he really wishes to become, deep down in his soul. This is how he really feels he is. It's his Ideal of himself. Man as metaphor, rather than meat. A dream figure.'

'There's plenty of meat on Geneva,' said Frank.

'So that was her secret dream. To be an Amazon, a titan. It was her soul's dream, unknown even to her.'

'And Mr King's dream was to be a fairy?'

'That was his soul's dream. He wished to be utterly beautiful – and, gosh,' for Shiba favoured slipping one or two British idioms into his speech, 'he is too. But not by any ordinary standards of good looks. No, this is the beauty of a humming-bird, or a butterfly. I'll wager that if *you*, Mr Caldero, were injected with the virus then you wouldn't turn out to be anything like either of them. You might become a werewolf or . . . oh, I don't know what! Something aquatic, breathing water. A merman, maybe. A *kappa*: Japanese frog-boy.'

'Speak for yourself,' thought Frank.

'Look,' he said, 'all the rats ended up resembling each other physically. Ditto with the chimps.'

'Ah, but rats have *cunning* as their dream. While monkeys have dexterity – that's theirs. But with us . . . Animals haven't got as much imagination as human beings.'

'Frankly, I'd say that the superchimps are somewhat *less* agile now! Especially when they walk.'

'No, no. Their hands are extremely agile and expressive. The dexterity resides in the hands. With us, as I was saying, our human imagination comes into play. It seems as though the world is newly made, and we can recreate ourselves according to our heart's desire. Yet this remains an unknown desire. We can't command it. We can't fore-guess it. None of us knows what he or she really desires. Yet something knows. Maybe it's the body cells – or the subconscious. Our change is a mythological force, Mr Caldero! And this is the real dream of mythology. It's the way back to the wonderful magical race of sirens and harpies and manticoras, of *kappa* and *ningyo*, the Japanese mermaid. Everyone will become his or her own species! This virus is a soul-teratogen.'

'Come again?'

'A breeder of monsters, from out of the soul. Yet they're perfectly viable monsters. They're beautiful, each in its own terms. Gosh!'

'I suppose that's one way of looking at it.'

'It'll be Mr King's way of looking at it. I know it will.'

'Do you really think he'll be *glad* to turn into a fairy? Lord, let's hope so. As I see it, Dr Ohira, this whole project has just gone sweetly up the spout.'

'Oh no. No.'

'How are they going to *mate*, for Chrissake?'

Ohira waved a hand impatiently.

'To make their super-children? Ah, that's less important now. Other people will join in this, this *wonderland* by invitation. With Mr King's consent, of course. Brave and bold spirits will beg to be admitted. Oh, I can see it now! Naturally, you'll have to be just as discreet in your recruitment programme as you were in hiring Jean Sandwich originally.'

'Are you crazy? We can't go out and *advertise* this!'

'Mr King will be requiring unusual company, won't he?'

'I don't see why. "Two Paradises 'twere in one, To live in Paradise alone,"' quoted Frank.

'Is that a proverb?'

'Listen: it isn't up to *you* to crowd the Farm out with . . .' With what? Freaks?

'I shall certainly raise the matter with Mr King when he wakes up. Given a big estate like this, it's only sensible. I have not heard Geneva worrying about her Swiss bank account lately.'

'Can you visualize her boarding a 747 to zoom off to Zürich? They'd have to tear a row of seats out. I'll give you a real proverb, Doctor: "Two's company."'

'If Mr King cannot have a family, he will need a community.'

'Damn it, that isn't what this project was about! It was about – '

'It could very well be about that now.' And Ohira eyed Frank speculatively.

Frank challenged him. 'I'll tell you what you'd really like. You'd like to see a huge *bonsai* garden – consisting of people. A garden of freaks, warped by your virus. You've been bitten by the collecting bug.'

'Warped? Ah, not by *my* skill, but by the souls of those concerned. Please remember, Mr Caldero: it's your garden too. You love it passionately, perhaps? You'd love to live in it always, wouldn't you? I have seen jealousy written on your face.'

Chapter 10

Bruno King grew slighter and even more beautiful before he awoke. Two filmy, ballooning membranes sprouted between his arms and his sides, extending from wrist to waist. These were angel wings, though attached like the webs of some gliding mammal.

Ohira had gone once into the changing room, wearing protective clothing, to examine these wings. When he handled the comatose body, he received a fierce electric shock; his arm was paralysed for half an hour.

On the twelfth day of the metamorphosis Ohira halted the soporific drug. Wearing thick-soled rubber boots and rubber gloves this time, he successfully disconnected the plumbing from the fairy's arms, mouth, nostrils, penis and anus. Either the rubber insulated him perfectly, or else the unconscious body sensed that no unnecessary meddling was intended. No shock was discharged.

The following morning, Bruno King (that was) sat up and saw himself.

He stared in amazement, with great dewy eyes. The mirror returned his image. He warbled joyously, and pranced about the room. His membranes inflated like twin arm-parachutes, allowing him momentarily to defy gravity.

Now he was a fairy kite: something which children might fly on a summer's day high on the end of a string. Yet he was both child *and* kite at once. This was his transfiguration, dreamed long ago, and long forgotten, back in the dawn days of his life before the paper of the kite became all one colour: green, printed with bank serial numbers.

'How do you feel, sir?' Frank was worried in case another surge of electricity might conduct down the kite string from out of the heavens which King now inhabited.

Perhaps the new King couldn't talk, thought Frank. Perhaps he could only warble. Frank patted his pocket, in which reposed the packet of envelopes, each marked '*In the Event of* . . .'

Yet the fairy's voice was a joy to hear. It was lyrical; it was a song.

'Geneva doesn't *need* all that money!' he trilled. 'She already has all she needs.'

This was like his old voice. Yet whereas it had always sounded shrill and twangy before, now it was trained and tuned and pure. The voice matched the pixy body perfectly.

'She must know that by now! Let me out, let me out into the grounds!'

Ohira smiled smugly. Even so, he held up a warning hand.

'What is it, man?'

'Just *one* moment, sir. Are you aware that you can deliver a powerful electric shock? A shock strong enough to stun a man, or maybe even kill him?'

The pixy considered this for a moment. Briefly his body crackled with static, as he thought of it.

'Yes, yes, it's quite true! How remarkable! Thank you for drawing it to my attention. Here, Ohira, let me show you.' He thrust out his little hand. 'Don't worry, it's under voluntary control.'

Gingerly Ohira extended a hand. (Once shocked, twice shy.) Fingers touched. Nothing happened.

'I'll give you a tiny little demonstration shock now – are you ready?'

Ohira yelped, and jerked back.

'Aw, that was nothing. Don't be so soft.'

The doctor shook his fingers about as if knocking mercury back down an invisible thermometer. He winced.

'How do you, hmm, do it?'

'Not telling. Why should I? I hold all the patents here. Now, kindly let me *out*. I'm getting impatient.'

McKinnon and Maccoby had bunched by the window, on alert, shouldering each other like defence tacklers.

'You aren't strong enough to open the door yourself,' thought Frank. 'Yet on the other hand . . . *Shazam!* You can knock a man down.'

'You won't be able to bowl Geneva over with electric shocks,' he remarked. 'It would take a cannon to knock her out.'

'That isn't exactly how I envisage it, Caldero!' The pixy King leapt high in the air. 'Maccoby, open the doors! Right now!'

'Yes, Mr King,' came a shout through the glass.

'King, no more,' declared the one-time Bruno. 'Except to people on the outside. To all the rest of you, I'm Ariel now. You will call me Ariel.'

The inner door swung open.

An hour later, Frank and Ohira and Maccoby watched through binoculars as Ariel came gliding in from some maple trees to land on Geneva's mighty shoulder.

He whispered in her ear. The giantess laughed merrily, and plucked him from her shoulder. While Maccoby tensed, as if to run and rescue him, she tossed Ariel high in the air. He glided around her, and around again in a figure eight, to land upon her once again, and bend as though to sip at her breasts.

The ill-assorted pair – the great troll woman and the sprite – seemed to be getting on famously together. Frank would have gone so far as to say that they were in love, at first sight; more so, indeed, than if there had been some rambunctious thrashing about of randy Titans. They were in love with *what* they were.

That night the two changed people did not return to the Farm buildings. What they were up to, or where, no one knew.

Geneva checked in the next morning, ravenous for steaks. Ariel, perching on her shoulder, demanded a bowl of milk and honey.

Chapter 11

The idyll lasted for all of two weeks. But then, even without being prompted by Ohira, Ariel grew restless. At least, Frank did not *think* that Ohira had prompted him . . .

The couple had taken up permanent nightly abode in one of the several temples scattered about the estate: appropriately enough, the Temple of Venus. Deep in an oakwood, this particular temple was decorated with erotic frescoes which Frank knew well from his former wanderings. Upon the walls beasts and half-beasts copulated with human beings, while up on the ceiling was painted the ingenious frame in which Pasiphaë seduced a bull in rut, to conceive the Minotaur. Frank couldn't help wondering whether Ariel and Geneva were using these frescoes as their personal *Kama Sutra*, searching for a suitable fit between 'hare' man and 'elephant' woman.

One morning Ariel flitted in from the wild, while Geneva waited for him by the yew-hedge maze. He convened a conference out in the open air, consisting of Frank and the Japanese doctors, Robina Weber, McKinnon and Maccoby, and Major (Joe) Lambert, the Farm Manager . . .

'It isn't enough,' chirped Ariel. 'I need more to occupy me.'

'We could smuggle you back to the penthouse, without anyone being any the wiser,' suggested Frank. 'I suppose John Schaeffer might insist on seeing you. But there's always the precedent of Howard Hughes . . .'

'Stop babbling, Frank. I want volunteers.'

Ohira clapped politely, like a Chinese leader applauding himself at an airport.

'Quite right, Sir Ariel. The experiment must broaden its scope, *né*?'

Major (Joe) Lambert spoke up. Major Lambert was a podgy, balding man with long blond moustaches and thick blond eyebrows.

'Really, this ain't the sort of thing my boys and girls would go for. It's sort of spooky and unsettling, what's going on here, see what I mean? 'Course, it doesn't bother *me*, sir. And *they* don't gossip when they're on furlough, no sir! This is another Los Alamos to them. 'Far as they're concerned, it's a *Government* project – and for all I know, it *may* be too. You're experimenting with alien beings in that monkey house. You've captured a UFO crew.'

Robina smirked.

'Quite right, Major. Of course we have.'

'That's the safest attitude.'

'I have a suggestion, sir,' said Maccoby. 'The rest of the estate ought to be sealed off now. With your permission I'll install communications gear up in that temple of yours. That way you won't risk freaking the employees.'

'Good thinking, Reuben.'

'I'll see to it today. But going beyond that, what Joe says about *his* staff doesn't exactly apply to mine. I recruited those guards – they've seen weirder things. But *they* aren't volunteer material. Not for that. They need to stay high and clear, to do their job properly. Anyway, I need them all.'

'There's a matter of inducement,' said Frank.

'What are you thinking of?' cried Ariel. 'A million in cash for my beloved Geneva was *one* thing. She was the first brave pioneer. But no way am I going to pay a million to all comers. Not now that the thing's *proven*. So come up with a better idea.'

'Fifty thousand – '

'No, no. The experience is its own reward.'

'Well sure, but how do we put that over? I mean, *you* say so,' Frank added carelessly, 'but I wouldn't know, would I?'

A gleam entered Ariel's eye.

'I mean, obviously I could "persuade" assorted bums and hobos,' Frank hurried on. 'But you mightn't like what they changed into.'

'On the contrary, I should rejoice to see the despised and disadvantaged ennobled! Geneva was one such. And to tell the truth, so was I. I intend the world to be reshaped.'

'You really want me to kidnap winos off the streets? You want to fill the place with satyrs?' Thought Frank: some of those frescoes really *have* affected him . . .

'Would you rather I keep more select company? Ah Frank, *try* to perceive the shape of the future: every man his own dream, every woman hers. A thing like this has to grow, Frank, or else it falls down. It's just like business – a simple matter of dynamics. One thing I haven't forgotten is the goal I set myself – just because I turned out, to my amazement and delight, to be this wonderful being, Ariel.'

'Oh yes . . . the goal . . . of course. The super-race. Well, *I* hadn't forgotten that either, sir. But have you and Geneva . . .? I mean, *can* you and Geneva – ?'

'Can we cut the mustard? Oh Frank, I have had my eyes opened. What I dreamed of before was just a human fantasy of firmer muscles, brighter brain, perhaps a few wild talents.' ('He's using my name too often,' thought Frank uneasily.) 'But I'm transhuman now. As is Geneva, my beloved. We have gone beyond. You can no more describe our present condition to the uninitiated than you can describe the act of riding a bicycle. It simply has to be experienced. So who will experience the change next?'

McKinnon and Maccoby both folded their arms. Major (Joe) Lambert twiddled his moustaches. Robina signed to herself with one hand, and replied with the other. Dr Ohira adopted the mask of a benign Buddha.

Arriving like an avalanche, Geneva was abruptly in their midst. Scooping Ariel up on to her shoulder, she pointed a finger squarely at Frank.

Ariel twittered in her ear. She boomed back at him. Twitter and boom, for a while. Frank couldn't – didn't dare – understand. Then Ariel, from on high, announced:

'*You* will change, Frank. This is my gift to my bride. Afterwards of course, you will be our peer in every way. You can even have a temple, all of your own.'

Geneva grinned, crunchingly.

'I just want to show my gratitude, Frank, in the most appropriate way.'

'Hey! Wait a minute.'

'More like two weeks, than a minute.' Ohira polished his hands.

'For Chrissake, I'm supposed to be your attorney! Who'll keep in touch with Schaeffer at KEB?'

'Oh, I can easily run things from the Temple, as soon as Reuben fixes it up.'

'Consider it fixed up, sir.'

'And you'll still be able to help me, Frank. In between our other, richer occupations. As Founder of the Future, I can see there's a lot to be done.'

'But – '

'May your secret desire be fulfilled!' Ariel clapped his hands gleefully; a few sparks flew.

'Look at it this way, sir: there's *two* of you – '

'Three, quite soon.'

' – versus four or five *billion* normal people! I mean, I can imagine a superman who looks approximately normal founding a new race, you know, as a long-term project, and getting away with it. I mean, that *was* the idea – '

'Clearly the superman concept was fundamentally in error,' Ohira said primly.

'Right!' Ariel clapped his hands again, showering sparks. 'This is the *dawn* time come round again. This is the time when forms were fresh and whimsical. It's the dream time. That's what's been waiting in us all these ages – to *save* us. Save us – yes! Changing is going to be our salvation. This will bring Heaven down to Earth. It'll be a *religious* force, but it'll be nothing like that God Nut crap. And *that's* how I'll swing the future. This is going to be like the old Greek religion. Thou art defeated, O pale Galilean.'

'But all that Greek religious stuff was just myth.'

'Myth is the *truth*. It's this world that's a sham. Here on my estate rises the new Olympus.'

'But you'll get clobbered. Stomped on. You can't set up a centre for changes as though it was some sort of acupuncture booth or Scientology bureau. It's illegal. Shit, it's *so* illegal. The God Nuts will tear the Farm to pieces – even before the Government get a chance to close you down.'

'I do have resources, Frank. We'll orchestrate this all neatly. Together. I simply need my little band of true disciples first: people who are thoroughly converted, soul and body.'

'But who'll go talent-spotting for you, if I'm – ? No, this is ridiculous. It isn't happening.'

'Have *I* not happened? Has Geneva not happened?'

'This has got to be kept *private*. You're crazy.' Frank fumbled the packet of envelopes from his pocket.

Maccoby stepped over and neatly lifted the packet from his grasp, then began to shred it.

'*I* believe in Mr Ariel.'

Frank started to run.

'Don't be foolish!' came Ariel's cry.

'Hey, hold on there!' called Major (Joe) Lambert.

Frank feared that Geneva might come thundering after him, but she didn't. He ran off in the direction of the garages, next to the main ranch house.

Maccoby blew a whistle.

'Chimp *squad*!' he bellowed.

A siren went off in the guard tower. Alerted by it, two more guards spilled out of the games complex, clutching rifles. No, those were anaesthetic dart guns. The guards halted, puzzled, when they saw Frank and not an escaping superchimp.

'*He's* the chimp!' shouted McKinnon. 'Caldero's the monkey!'

Obediently the guards moved to head Frank off.

Frank changed direction, and ended up by running around in a complete circle which brought him back towards the maze.

This was one devil of a maze. A few months ago, after numerous earlier attempts, Frank had finally reached the centre and memorized the correct route. At the centre he had discovered a flagstone with a ring in it. Beneath the flagstone, a flight of stone steps descended into blackness. He hadn't a torch with him at the time, and he hadn't been back since, but no doubt these steps joined the tunnel which linked the Farm buildings with the atom-bomb-proof cavern under the uplands of the state.

Neither Maccoby nor McKinnon, nor Geneva for that matter, bothered to cut him off – as they so easily could have done – when he sprinted past them. They merely stood laughing as he dodged through the entry gap in the thick high hedges, pursued by the two riflemen ten yards behind.

He ran, ducking low so that the guards up in the watchtower would not see him except when he rounded corners.

Left here. Now right. And left again. And left again . . .

Frank made twenty choices and believed he was still on course. But then two openings presented themselves, side by side. He stopped, unsure.

On the other side of the hedge, he heard footsteps pounding. But that didn't matter! The other side couldn't – mustn't! – connect with this side.

Choosing the nearer entry, he chased after the footsteps which were now departing. Very soon he diverged from them, plunging deeper into the labyrinth.

That had been one set of footsteps. So the guards had split up.

Which only meant that one of them would be completely lost by now; their chances of catching and subduing him were halved. He listened, and ran on.

Perhaps five minutes passed.

A shrill cry, from the tower. 'There he is!'

Skidding in the cinders, Frank ducked around a corner then peered back.

Geneva was holding Ariel out of one of the windows on the lookout cabin. While Frank watched, she launched the sprite. Ariel's membrane ballooned, and he glided down swiftly across the maze. He was not holding any dart gun, though. Too heavy for him.

Frank dashed through another entrance, and another.

Thirty feet up, Ariel circled and spotted him again. The sprite dropped down out of sight.

'So I'm getting close,' thought Frank. 'Too close for his comfort!'

He ran round another corner and collided with the hedge. He was in a cul-de-sac. For a moment he fought with the hedge, trying to force his way through. But the yew was unyielding. Besides, the path on the other side was probably *further* away from the centre. Hastily he backtracked, and took another opening.

Another.

Suddenly he ran into the open square at the centre of the maze . . .

Ariel sat perched on the stone slab, with one hand on the ring.

'Frank, Frank, *behave* yourself!'

'Would you just mind shifting off that stone . . . sir?'

'But I do mind. It's my stone.'

'I'll have to shift you myself, then. Sir.'

'Oh, *Frank*.'

Without thinking, Frank seized Ariel by the arm. And immediately a sledgehammer hit him.

In his anxiety to escape, Frank had quite forgotten that Ariel's body was a heavy-duty battery.

A while later he discovered that he was lying on his back, staring up at the sky through a vortex of rotating hedges. He heard voices.

'How the – ?' (Panting.)

Ariel's silvery tones: 'Oh, I have the magic touch. Now put a dart into him, there's a good fellow.'

Spectres pranced around amidst the swirling hedges: ogres and centaurs and hobgoblins . . . Which of them would he become? Surely now was the time to choose, if choosing had anything to do with it.

'Shazam!' he wished. 'Oh Shazam!'

A bee seemed to sting him in the leg, and thirty seconds later he was asleep.

Chapter 12

Of what happened next his conscious mind knew nothing; and when his senses were restored to him, he found himself in mind and body quite different from before . . .

Yet what dreams he had dreamt.

He had dreamed that the two Japanese doctors changed a fertilized human egg into a pine tree seed. This they planted, and as soon as it grew into a seedling they proceeded to cultivate this seedling as a *bonsai*. Amputating most of its roots, they repotted it in a tight bowl packed with a sharp sand mixture to sting the remaining threadling roots. They wired it tortuously so that it groaned as it grew – becoming a tiny twenty-year-old pine, bowed and gnarled. Whereupon they changed it back into a person, and this person was a dwarf, an ugly gnome – hunchbacked, covered with warts. They had snipped his roots all too energetically, for this dwarf possessed no toes. He could only stomp about awkwardly on the stumps of his feet.

He dreamed that Ohira and Shiba changed other human eggs into cactus seeds. These grew into red-blooded cacti with no chlorophyll in them at all. They were that freak of the cactus family: *Gymnocalycium mihanowiczii Friedrichiae* var. '*Hibotan*', little red tubs with chins under all the spines. The doctors grafted these shrieking scions on to green cactus stock, and when they were fully grown changed them back into hedgehog-men and porcupine-women – short, rotund people bristling with quills and spines . . .

He dreamed of the doctors pursuing their experiments still further, changing animals and people into plants, then grafting these together to produce weird hybrids (when they were changed back later on), such as a centaur, a harpy, a sphinx, a mermaid, a manticora . . .

In addition, they also cultivated the Vegetable Lamb of Tartary – a gourd-bearing plant, the fruit of which ripened to give birth to tiny sheep. From this, they moved on to hybridize sunflowers which grew up to bloom with human faces, petals in place of yellow hair.

In his dreams Frank had gradually been adopting the perspective of the plants themselves.

The dreams faded reluctantly, trying to cling to his mind like ivy.

He opened his eyes.

The hand which he lifted was a normal shade of green, familiar from his dreams. The skin hardened at his wrist, into brown bark, on which grew a certain healthy amount of lichen. As he shifted, the trunk of his body creaked – though really it was quite limber and mobile. His rutted brown legs bent at his command, as he sat up. He observed that his feet (with their horny toenails, most suitable for digging holes) were covered in thick grey hairs and tendrils rather like dirty polar bear boots. They itched to sink into damp, soft soil.

His raised hand brushed his head, and he discovered that his hair had thickened and spread into green blades.

He glanced round the changing room. The two Japanese. Behind the glass panel, Geneva, with Ariel riding buoyantly on her shoulder . . . He found the fluorescent lighting insubstantial – impoverished, somehow. It wasn't real daylight. He almost went back to sleep. With an effort, he marshalled his resources. If he didn't get out into real daylight soon, he would go comatose. If his feet didn't tread dirt, he would dry out.

His hand strayed down to his nose. It had become a mere woody knob. He certainly wasn't breathing through it. For a moment or two this discovery panicked him, till he realized how ridiculous it would be to breathe through a mere couple of holes, when his whole body could breathe through every pore.

To compensate for this atrophy of his nose, he had a great cavity of a mouth. As soon as he hinged it open – almost splitting his head in half – a heady perfume drifted out. Shiba began to walk forward, sniffing, a dazed look in his eyes. Hurriedly Ohira plucked at his colleague and made him tighten the surgical mask which had been hanging loose around his chin.

Ohira stepped back and clapped politely.

'It's just as I said: *Homo Sylvestris* – Tree-Man! What a wonderful adaptation to living in the wilds. But I wonder how it breeds? By seed, or by suckers? It's scent is intoxicating, *né*? I smell danger there, Shiba-*sensei*. I think this may well be a carnivorous tree.'

Frank (that was) understood Ohira easily, though he suspected that the brain which processed these sentences was perhaps no longer in the same location as before, but in a safer place. Or distributed around his new body in several locations.

He considered his mouth, gullet and belly; he visualized the deep tube and the digestion vat of a pitcher plant.

'Dual feeding mode,' went on Ohira happily. 'Roots and leaves, *plus* mouth. But can it talk?'

Frank wondered about his genitals, and his hand strayed to his crotch. Where his scrotum had once been, now there was another woody knob with a pipe of soft wood like a whistle resting on it. Perhaps his whistle still worked, though, even though it had lignified.

He must look as though he was just sitting there, greenly masturbating. Or attempting to. Realizing this, he removed his hand and stood up creakingly. His feet tried to dig into the floor, but the tiles were too smooth and hard. If he stamped down firmly enough, maybe he could break them. But what was underneath? Concrete? He resisted the impulse.

'Can you talk, Frank?'

'Frank . . . ?' He pondered the name.

Yes, he did know perfectly well who 'Frank' had been. Frank was the pattern of tree-rings throughout his body: thirty-five yearly growth rings arranged like the grooves on a long-playing record. Except that the arrangement wasn't a spiral; it was year by year. Thirty-five successive tracks, one for each of his years. He played the most recent grooves back to himself.

'Shazam!' squealed the stylus.

'I can recognize a *Monstera Deliciosa* when I see one . . .'

'Two Paradises 'twere in one . . .'

It was all old wood.

'Yes, I can talk.' His voice gurgled, somewhat. 'Look, I must get out into the daylight. Or I'll go dormant. I have to sink my roots for a while, or I'll wither.'

'You need to plant yourself somewhere?'

The tree-man considered this.

'Not permanently. I'm ambulatory. I'll roam all over the loam. Look, fellows, I have to get outside.' And Frank (that was) stomped towards the door.

'You'll notice that he doesn't give off that scent while he's speaking. His speech organs must seal off the tunnel to his stomach. Or wherever the scent glands are.'

Frank (that was) paused.

'I've lost my lungs,' he glugged. 'I can breathe all over me.'

'*Excellent* adaptation! Though it must slow him down a little, *né*?'

'Maybe not,' suggested Shiba. 'Larger surface area – direct oxygen access.'

'Ah, but by osmosis, from the surface inwards. No, I'd say the system must inevitably be slower. We can easily find out. Frank, with your permission – once you've adjusted to your, hmm, natural habitat – we'd like to put you through your paces, say, on a running belt.'

'*Sensei*, I think he has a *liquid* voice box, twanged by vibration. While it's in use it seals the gullet.'

Frank (that was) nodded his crown.

'Something like that.'

Gripping the handle, he wrenched the door open and presently lurched through into the observation room.

Ariel landed on his shoulder, just where his right-hand bough branched out.

'Beaut-i-ful!' he trilled. 'You've excelled yourself! I knew you *wood*.'

Grinning, Geneva thumped the tree-man resoundingly on the back; and though the blows would have felled the earlier Frank, now they only rocked him about.

'Got to get *outside*,' he insisted. 'Can't stay indoors. It's like being buried alive.'

'The open air for me,' cried Ariel, 'the naked soil for you. Come along.'

Maccoby eyed the tree-man with a mixture of wonder, amusement and distress.

'Sir, I don't think the ordinary guys ought to see this one. I think we should drive him some way out in the pick-up, with a sack over him.'

'That's reasonable. But not a sack – that's too constricting. A tarpaulin. Wait a moment: can you climb on board a truck, Frank?'

Frank (that was) raised one foot about a hand's span above the floor, with an effort, then hastily stood down again.

'Won't be easy.'

'You'd better bring the truck with the loading platform, Reuben. If that's away at the moment, drive a fork-lift over.'

Nodding, Maccoby departed on his errand.

'Not long now, Frank,' whispered Ariel into the leafy knot-hole in the side of the changed man's head. 'Just be patient. You're a wonder – a marvel.'

'Does that make me *Captain* Marvel?'

But Frank (that was) felt very remote from his early fantasies of Clark Kent and Billy Batson. That was just a silly ambition, graven in the rings of yesteryear – the product of a younger, more foolish season. The tree-man laughed to remember it.

'Might I suggest a new name, if nothing special springs to mind? I mean, *I* knew I was Ariel immediately.'

'*Silvester*,' said . . . Silvester. 'That's who I am.'

'Excellent!'

And that was who he was.

Maccoby was back inside ten minutes. Draping a tarpaulin over

Silvester, Maccoby and Geneva guided the tree-man out to the waiting truck. The lifting platform whined, bearing him aloft. Steadied by Geneva, Silvester edged forward and stood in silence. How he yearned to put down roots and go to sleep. But the floor of the truck was steel. Some dried mud and hay teased and frustrated him.

Hardly had the truck started out, than it halted again. Silvester heard muffled voices, then the trundle of a gate rolling aside. For a moment or two he thought that they were taking him into the superchimp compound, to plant him there below in the subterranean sunshine. He jerked a branch angrily against the side of the truck. Then he remembered that the wilds of the estate had been sealed off too, by now.

In spite of the bumpiness of the ride, he was very nearly comatose by the time the truck halted for the second time. Geneva whipped off the tarpaulin, showering him with daylight.

He roused, and turned slowly.

As he edged woozily on to the platform, he felt sure that he wouldn't always be so vulnerable to sudden darkness. Just so long as he could spend all of the daylight hours soaking up and storing energy, he should easily be able to march around for several hours after sunset, if he chose. At the moment, on this first day, he was still relatively as weak as a sapling.

Chapter 13

It did not take Silvester long to discover that all his previous appreciation of the estate had amounted to little more than an exercise in nostalgia. He hadn't ever really touched or tasted the land. Hills, lakes and temples alike had merely been stand-ins for memories of his boyhood, when he had haunted the cypresses and hedgerows, the tombs and wildernesses of his local cemetery, dreaming of free space and the future. Undeniably that demi-paradise of his boyhood days had pointed forward to its later analogy, Bruno King's estate, yet equally the later analogy had only pointed back again, thus forming a fairly sterile loop in time: a reflection of a reflection.

Now that he could actually bury his roots in the soil, becoming a living part of the domain, before electing to move on to another favoured spot, he experienced the world directly for the first time.

Breezes caressed his hair-leaves; sun warmed his bark. He tasted the sparkle of dew, more effervescent than asti spumante. Worms tickled him, and so did other roots, some of them feelers from the great oaks themselves.

True, he did not commune directly with other trees, on their own level. Ordinary trees inhabited a plane of sensation that was to his, as theirs was to a boulder's. Yet by the same token he was able to evade the strangling knots and insidious, thirsty invasions of roots questing out from the other permanent trees. Their vegetable processes were so much slower than his own.

He could appreciate the activities of all the other plants as slow ballet – or as an equation whose factors were thirst, sun-lust, seed-lust and survival, yet whose solution was perfect beauty. Whenever he rooted himself in a meadow of buttercups and poppies, or amidst purple monkshood and the peering, sightless faces of field pansies, or within sight of sweet pink clover and tufted violet vetch and sunny ragwort, it appeared at first that here was simply a gratuitous explosion of loveliness, to daze the bees and butterflies. Yet he felt the undertow of competition, too. And could stay clear of it, simply admiring the ballet – and the ballet dresses. The ballet was conducted at various *tempi*, ranging from quite slow to extremely slow; and at last a mind, Silvester's, had joined in.

Of course, even an ordinary tree had little to worry about, saving maybe an infestation of ivy, mistletoe or bindweed, and hardly even then. And even an ordinary tree did not 'worry' in any nervous sense . . .

Since he was much shorter than any tree of equivalent girth, Silvester wondered whether eventually he would grow as tall as the best of them and so become a walking giant: a giant far greater than Geneva, whose footfalls shook the world, whose steps pressed holes into the meadows.

Yet if that happened, he doubted that he could possibly remain mobile. Surely the laws of mechanics would anchor him, rooting him deep, spreading his weight like a wooden octopus extending its arms. So long as he continued to uproot himself and march about, he was in effect performing a *bonsai* operation upon himself . . .

His perception of time had changed, too. Now, from dawn to dusk, each day was a model in miniature of the whole round of the seasons from spring to winter. Every day he underwent the whole cycle of ripening and retreating. Thus every day seemed to be now, forever. Yet he also remembered the past, as lignified in his rings. And he believed that he would begin to know the future too, simply because no other brain could possibly know the *present* as keenly as he knew it. All other minds were the puppet prisoners of past memories. Whereas time had been liberated for Silvester.

And if one day he should grow tired of roaming and of tasting new terrain? Then he would choose an advantageous spot where he could send down permanent roots. Such a spot would have to be out of the north wind, though not somewhere where he might be overgrown. And in this chosen place he would meditate for centuries – as other trees, in a sense, meditated – and he would become, if he retained the power of speech, an oracle. A tree oracle.

Ah yes! People of the future would flock to his sacred grove. They would gird his trunk around with a ceremonial rope on which they would hang waxed red paper butterflies, and prayers, and other offerings. Silvester would utter his oracles from high up, out of a vent which he always kept open in himself, in a groaning voice (as of boulders grinding in a mountain stream in flood). And so he would predict the traceries of change branching through a world remade.

Would actual sacrifices be made to him? Would hot reeking meat be raised to his open mouth on poles?

As well as soaking up sun and dew and the minerals dissolved in the soil, Silvester was also carnivorous . . .

Did his mobility, in fact, depend upon his eating flesh? Would it be said one day of the great oracle tree: 'Only the tree that eats, can speak'?

Shaking his dew-heavy leaves from his eyes, he scattered spray around him which rainbowed briefly in the morning sun; and silently he yawned. Yawned wide.

Musk drifted forth upon the breeze.

Soon, a fat thrush flew whistling to him. The bird was intoxicated, dreaming of nestlings clamouring to be fed, of a snake-knot of juicy worms, of the love-pang of mating. She dived promptly down Silvester's throat.

He clapped shut his wooden mouth. The thrush drowned in delight.

After a while he opened his trap again. This time a blackbird dived in.

While he absorbed the two birds, his leaves were rustling like feathers.

He still felt hungry.

A squirrel scampered up his bark and popped inside him. Down his gullet it scuttled on sharp claws to splash into the sticky reservoir. Soon, for a while, he felt what it was like to wear a bushy tail to balance you.

Presently waste bled from the pipe in his crotch, staining his bark yellow. Gently uprooting himself, he set out to return to the Temple of Venus. But he should wade through a stream *en route* to wash himself.

The evening before, Geneva and Ariel had sequestered themselves as usual in their temple, with its heavy Ionic portico and its Palladian quadrants. Silvester had continued to loiter close by, wondering still about their method of love-making.

So he had eavesdropped on Geneva's cries and lowings of ecstasy, distinguishing these easily from other night sounds: such as the hooting of an owl, or the yip and howl of a couple of foxes.

Overcome with curiosity, he had at last mounted the single low step of the portico and banged his right-hand branch against the door: twice, and twice again.

Abrupt silence had followed this woody boom.

In his gurgling voice he had called out.

A while had passed before Geneva, naked, sweaty and languorous, hurled the door open. (It was quite characteristic of her that even in her most languorous state she had hurled open the door.)

On the edge of an outsize ottoman draped with sheepskin rugs in disarray, perched Ariel. His body glowed like a will o' the wisp. This light picked out (faintly) the erotic murals and the communications console and computer terminal, as well as a stone cornucopia filled with avocado pears and tomatoes. The gutted carcass of a Muntjac deer hung from a hook. Other hooks supported a hare, a heavy trout, and many gourd-like salamis, mortadellas and wursts. The inside of the temple was a blend of boudoir, command centre, and butcher's shop, with a touch of fishmonger. It smelt of meat, musk and electric ozone.

Geneva had flexed herself sensuously, her sides of meat and muscle rippling.

'Are you coming in, or not?'

'Yes, do come in!' Ariel had invited. 'Would you like some honeyed milk?'

'Water is best, for a tree.' Silvester shuffled about on his horny root-pads. 'I don't much like standing on bare stone.'

Spinning about, Geneva had jerked two sheepskins off the couch so swiftly that Ariel stayed sitting in approximately the same position as before. Walter Raleigh-like, she had spread these on the floor in front of Silvester. He had shuffled on to them, and as though with a mind of their own his roots had begun writhing into the wool.

'I want to ask you . . . I want to know about love. About sex, to be precise. How do you two *do* it? I've been wondering.'

Geneva had unhooked a hefty garlic sausage and chomped a great bite out of the seasoned phallus, filling her mouth. She chewed noisily.

Ariel grinned impishly.

'Well, anything for a friend! We make love *electrically*, you see!'

Abruptly he had hopped up on to the back of the ottoman and launched himself at Geneva. His little legs had clamped around her neck. His arms, with their membrances fully flared, were now wrapped around her neck. Though his glow had been fading fast, he blazed alight again.

'Uuunnnggg,' Geneva moaned, shaking her head and its rider from side to side. Ariel trembled on top of her.

'I discharge my power,' he had gasped, 'into her pleasure centres.' Flipping upside down, he had squirrelled down her body, seeking hand holds on her nipples, in her navel, in her crotch hair. 'And the nerves themselves: those I feed directly. Mainly the erogenous nerves. I can pleasure any nerve, or pain it. And it *pleases* me, when I discharge. Oh, it pleases me!'

He had dropped down to the floor in a monkey crouch; and Geneva had rocked back.

'You must have liked it when you knocked that Frank Caldero

out,' said Silvester. As soon as he said this, he had realized that he was referring to himself – but really, it was another self, a self that had been absorbed: a foetus turned to a pod of dead wood in the womb, or melted back into sap. He had realized, too, that Ariel was saying that he could equally well be a sadist if he chose. He did not so choose.

'I need to *earth* myself. If I don't, well, I feel that I'll turn into a ball of lightning, and *explode*.'

Thus if Ariel was captured, thought Silvester, and if he was hung in a wooden cage – such as a cage of branches tightly woven together – then he would accumulate more and more charge until suddenly he burst . . .

'Maybe you wouldn't explode,' he suggested. 'Maybe you would just turn into a creature of pure energy. An energy being.'

'Maybe my *children* will be like that. Ah, children . . . I'm sure I can tickle the egg in the womb – yes, just like the first lightning striking the amniotic oceans of old Earth! I'll trigger a virgin birth, with my own imprint in the egg. That's what the old story of the angel fertilizing Mary means. But don't you see, what is born of such a union is energized *flesh*? I haven't worked out how to produce a pure energy being. Not yet. That's the nuisance: just three of us. We haven't a sufficient range of changed persons. Not yet. Oh, but there will be grades and grades of altered beings before long, *compadre*! There'll be aerial beings. And beast beings. There'll be vegetable beings and I don't know what else.'

'Grades? Do you mean, arranged like a hierarchy? With us vegetable-men at the bottom?'

'My fine Lord of the Trees, *all* have their precious place! All. We're aiming to build a transhuman *ecology*. Have I satisfied your curiosity enough?'

'Well, that's how you get *your* rocks off. But how about me?'

'Time will tell. Shall I leap into your branches and discharge myself, to see how it affects you?'

Silvester had drawn back.

'Trees don't much like being struck by lightning. Anyway, I might be a tree, but I'm not a *gay* tree.'

'How about trying it with female trees?' suggested Geneva brightly. She had now recovered from her nerve storm of ecstasy. 'Don't cherry trees have two sexes? Male and female?'

'But that would be bestiality!'

'You mean *arboreality*.'

'It would be like buggering a clothes horse! No, wait! That's unfair . . . I know what you mean. There's such sweet joy, being rooted in a woodland. Particularly when it's full of flowers. The bees buzzing about like tiny soft breasts. The butterflies like fluttering tattooed vulvas. Feeling the touch of other roots. Smelling the pollen . . . But I'm thinking I mightn't become sexually mature unless I take root permanently – and grow and grow! If I do, I'm sure I'll become an oracle tree. Maybe I'll copulate with *time* itself – with the unborn future. It's too soon for that – I still like walking about. Oh, but I do feel the power of prophecy growing in me!'

Despite himself, Silvester had yawned. But not because of the smell of rich meats. Excited though he felt, weariness was creeping over him. He shook himself and concentrated.

'More recruits!' he announced loudly. 'Conscripts, for freedom!' It was hard to say whether he was advising or predicting. At one time he remembered that he had been quite jealous at the prospect of sharing this estate with anyone. But trees tend to think in terms of forests: armies of other trees.

'When I *am* an oracle tree,' he mused, 'people will write their requests on paper darts and launch these into my mouth, for me to digest . . . Hell, that's nonsense! How could I possibly read the words in my belly? Besides, it's cannibalism. A tree can't possibly eat paper.'

Vague shadows of the future were assailing him, there in the darkened temple, lit only by the moon now that Ariel had dimmed. Silvester realized that it was easier to guess the future at night. By day sunshine blinded the vision of the future. Alas, he tended to be asleep at night.

He strove to peer into that enigmatic future. But he needed first to tap the earth for power and inspiration. Which, since it was night and cool and dark, would certainly send him into vegetable slumber.

'Maybe I shall dream the future, holding my petitioners cradled in my boughs, there embraced by me. Maybe that's how I'll copulate . . .

'But I'd be hungry in the morning. So they'd better watch out. They'd better wear nose-plugs or something.

'My petitioners will be roped to my mast, like Odysseus was! Their friends will drag them to safety in the morning . . .'

Pleased by this image, Silvester had stomped out through the portico and lurched down the single step on to turf and soil.

The temple door had banged behind him; though not before Ariel had called out a reminder about a planning meeting in the morning.

Somnambulistically Silvester had walked through the woods and up a moonlit meadow. Finally he reached a favoured spot. His roots writhed eagerly into the soil.

As he dozed off, he had felt that he was plugging into the world's unconscious. He felt sure that this undersoul was rising like a sap-stream – like a spring, to spill into all the rivers and the seas, and eventually to fall as raindrops upon everyone alive, magically altering them . . .

PART TWO
Argus

Chapter 14

'There is one unexamined aspect of the tale of Beauty and the Beast,' mused Rudolph. 'It's this: what if the Beast was more sexually exciting than the handsome Prince whom he became? What if the ugliness and the beastliness were authentically thrilling, whereas the Prince who emerged – like a dull moth out of a fiercesome caterpillar – was merely rather vapid and ordinary in his token good looks, once Beauty had got used to these?

'A few months after the false bliss of her wedding night, did Beauty find herself dreaming of the original true Beast mounting her? (Which indeed he had never tried to do, nor could ever do now.) Did that incubus rear itself in her subconscious, scorning the placid tenderness of their embraces? Did she feel subtly dissatisfied the morning after? Did a small voice still whisper, "Do not trust to appearances, Beauty"?'

'Did Beauty ever subsequently try to persuade her Prince to *dress up* in a beastly disguise – at some masked ball, say – and to take her bestially (even from behind) in a scullery or wood shed, thus to recapture the horrid delights the absence of which tormented her? That would have been a pretty romp indeed!

'And what if her Prince realized, when she opened her legs for him, that deep within her – deeper than *he* could reach – she cherished the memory of his former bestial self? Hairy, tusky, boarlike . . . a veritable Genghis Khan! (No, probably Genghis Khan sported willowy mandarin moustaches, and dressed in silks, and bathed in milk . . .)'

So mused Rudolph.

Rudolph was ugly.

Rudolph was disfigured.

His mother had known this the moment he was born. She spotted it instantly because she was such a perfect beauty herself. Even with her legs in the obstetric stirrups, no doubt the doctors desired her.

And Rudolph emerged, with this birthmark on his nose. A cherry.

The blemish was not tucked away in his armpit or on his buttocks or behind his shoulderblade. Had it been, then it could have awaited discovery by some fair woman during love play, as his personal hallmark, his secret seal; a dash of tabasco to add spice to their amorous games.

But it was right here, up front. Aglow. A red stop light to any such games, or any such love play. And a stop light to a lot of other things besides: to toddler socialization, to school rough and tumble, to normal friendship – a scar upon them all. A brand. If seen. If seen. And how could it not be seen?

His mother had intended all along to name him Rudolph, since she was crazy about old Valentino movies. Rudolph Rogers he would be. 'RR', intertwined, would look really neat as a monogram on his shirts. Like Rolls-Royce, indeed!

Mrs Rogers' tastes in music were somewhat along the lines of *The Desert Song*. Yet it must be presumed that at least one of the doctors in attendance at the delivery may tactfully have suggested that this particular name wasn't *quite* right for the baby – given the undeniable popularity of a certain other song about a red-nosed reindeer . . .

So she called him Richard instead.

Richard Rudolph Rogers.

Now, one may have supposed that 'Richard Rogers' was enough incense in itself to offer up to the Gods of Entertainment. But she was still crazy about Valentino.

The Gods . . . yes. Mrs Rogers was a worshipper. She wanted so very much to be a star. She had the looks. She had the figure. Alas, she didn't have the talent. And culturally, she was hopelessly out of date.

Nevertheless, she spent a small fortune of her husband's money – he was in real estate – and latterly of his alimony on talent schools and beauticians. As a result of which, she knew very well how to make lovely faces even lovelier. And she was not going to let her baby son (or, by extension, herself) be traumatized by that cherry mark.

As soon as Mrs Rogers and son were discharged from hospital, she carried Rudolph straight to a plastic surgeon, who explained that it wasn't possible (in effect) to cut off the boy's nose to favour his face. Nor would the cherry mark fade with time, as a lady doctor at the hospital had suggested by way of consolation. Mrs Rogers' boy was stuck with it forever.

So, at seven days old, commenced his life of disguise – of hidden beastliness.

On to his nose went cosmetics, not to enhance but to hide. After every evening bath, not only was his little body powdered but his nose was made up too.

Now, little babies – as everyone knows – tend to flap their rubbery fists around. Not so little Richard Rudolph. Mother measured out blue ribbons to tether his wrists decoratively so that he couldn't touch his face. She resolved that his hands would never stray up there except at the holy hour of the renewal of his disguise. But once that precious hour came around she actively encouraged him to participate; and the whole routine was reflected back at him from an overhead mirror, doubly to imprint him with the process of disguise.

So he grew up trained never to touch his face except in secret, at renewal time.

No doubt it was Mrs Rogers' insistence on this strict regime which alienated her husband, quite soon after the boy was born. Rogers Senior was so very used to showing strangers around houses, which are the shells of people's lives. It was a point of pride to him that no skeletons lurked in any cupboards. Now he couldn't even display his own son.

Rogers Senior avoided remarrying, in favour of less binding arrangements. Thus, when he crashed on a freeway just three years later – and he had been generously over-insured – the bulk of his insurance money went to his ex-wife. Mrs Rogers was set up for a life of nostalgia and cosmetic subterfuge.

As Richard Rudolph grew older, gradually he took over the responsibility for his own make-up. He needed to learn many other associated strategies, too. He had to overcome the sneezing reflex, whenever he had a cold. He must never go out in the rain. He must never get himself involved in any kiddy brawl which might result in a flailing hand blowing his cover away, revealing the awful cherry stain to staring eyes.

In a way his existence was far more difficult than that of, say, a child with no immune defences who has to be brought up in a sterile plastic tent. Unlike such a child, Rudolph had to interact with the ordinary world; even the private school to which his mother chauffeured him daily was a part of that ordinary world, however polite and tame it tried to be. At the same time he had to prevent the world from ever touching him in that one focal spot, the centre of his being. For at any moment he could be revealed as the Beast.

In a sense, then, he had no face. For his face was a mask, which no one must ever know to be a mask. As soon as he was seven years old, and judged by Mrs Rogers to be fully competent, thereafter not even *she* should be aware. From that time forth his own mother, who had guarded his beastly secret well, would keep it secret even from herself. They never spoke of it again. Whenever Rudolph needed to renew his own store of cosmetics he raided his mother's cabinet without a word. And he never disappointed her. He was wholly and safely 'Rudolph' now, to her. And to himself – the name had quite taken him over.

Yet of course a nose is more than merely a blob of flesh and gristle, through which you breathe. The most ancient part of the human brain is the olfactory lobe, the processor of smells. And this lobe evolved into the seat of the emotions, which in turn . . . well, quite literally the whole of the *rest* of the brain grew out of the nose.

Scientific studies have shown that when the penis swells, engorged with blood, so also does the nose – though to a lesser extent. The nose is a sort of penis on the face, and has been recognized as such since olden days. Big noses were always a sign of large members. A man who could sneeze explosively would enjoy a satisfying orgasm. In the fifteenth century the lustful Queen Julia of Naples chose only large-nosed lovers. The whole world knows about Cyrano de Bergerac.

Rudolph, who had successfully inhibited the sneezing reflex, had thus inhibited the orgasm too. As he grew into adolescence he discovered that he could never come, by the hand, except at that hour when his cosmetics were washed off prior to renewing his disguise. Only at that time of day, too, could he experience real emotions, or what he presumed were real emotions; only then, when the Beast was out, red as a ruby.

('The Beast' was by now his private name for his nose. Thus had he christened it: he who had never himself been christened, lest splashes of holy water should wash his cover away.)

He also had his most effective, creative thoughts at that hour when the Beast was loose. During the rest of the day his thinking was constrained and automatic, matching his routines of movement through the outside world.

When he was twenty-one, his mother died of lightning pneumonia. So perished the only other person who knew his awful secret – if indeed she *did* still know! (They hadn't discussed the matter for fourteen years.) And at last he was free of the irrational fear that one day she might feel tempted to betray him.

He was sole custodian of the Beast now; and a powerful Beast it was indeed, since not only was it in charge of his sexual delights but also of his flashes of high imaginative thought.

Increasingly it showed Rudolph how special he was compared to other people. Their lives, seemingly so spontaneous and unconstrained, were in fact deadly averaged out, with no peak moments to compare with his. Rudolph conserved all his energies for the naked hour. He stored up a whole day-long spool of data, thought and feeling, to let it rip in one ruby laser burst out into the cosmos each evening, as if he was communicating with some higher intelligence elsewhere in the universe – as if he was placed on Earth for this purpose.

Though, since nothing 'out there' replied, what then should he do with his secret power? What, upon *this* planet? On what mighty project should he focus his laser beam?

With the insurance money from his mother's death compounded with what was left over from his father's, he sought out and acquired a little old house deep in the country in the middle of a small wood, which he also bought. This new domain of his was near to a secret research facility (or so the whisper went locally), which was busy investigating UFOs and Ufonauts under the pretence of being merely the country estate of an eccentric billionaire who guarded his privacy fanatically.

If anybody could beam a message to a UFO, surely it was Rudolph! But he wasn't *naive*. So obviously he discounted the local rumours as a load of boondocks guff. The 'rich man's estate' just had to be a summer camp for spies, and maybe it also concealed a colony of safe houses: *dachas* for defectors. To be associated by proximity with it pleased him greatly; it was the best cover for his own plans. For if Rudolph was weird in his habits, well, so were they too. If they wanted to be left alone, well, equally so did he. He intended, as it were, to keep his nose clean.

(And indeed he had nosed around for weeks, employing all the acumen of Rogers Senior in his hunt for a place as suitable as this.)

Yet even in seclusion he did not intend to let his Beast roam freely around the woody domain. This would surely fritter its power away.

Instead, he brooded much upon the tale of Beauty and the Beast, determined to plumb its true symbolic depths. All fairy tales are really profound parables from the great Collective Unconscious, designed to guide people's conduct. The number of fairy tales is as huge as it is precisely because they must cover so many bizarre eventualities – including highly specialized states of being such as Rudolph's own – as well as the more ordinary workaday ones.

He was the Beast. But *where* was Beauty?

On a superficial reading of the story, Beauty ought to come and visit the Beast in his isolated retreat on account of some error on her father's part. Yet Rudolph already knew that the deep meaning of the tale would be concealed by a process of *inversion*. This is generally so, when the true meaning is unacceptable to ordinary mortals.

So did this mean that, rather than wait for Beauty to come to him, he should actively seek her out and bring her forcibly to his place despite all her father's well-laid schemes to guard her?

He would have to let his nose guide him on this. He unmasked the Beast, to let it decide.

As soon as the Beast was glowing, Rudolph immediately saw the trap of *banality* into which he had been about to plunge. Oh, the sheer ordinariness of kidnapping a Beauty and locking her up in the cellar of his house, there to become privy to his beastliness! His nose turned itself up in disgust at the idea. Here he was, in a privileged, exemplary position. So his solution must be a master stroke. It must be such as would only occur to an *initiate* of the story with all his wits about him, rather than someone who merely took it at face value.

Then his nose showed him the truth.

Chapter 15

The Beast could *see*. It could see by itself!

Rudolph had shut his eyes when he unmasked the Beast. This was the first time he had ever acted so at this holy moment. Every time before, he had stared fixedly at his face in the mirror, resisting even the urge to blink. Yet now he shut his eyes. And *this* was the master stroke.

For he could still see almost as clearly as ever.

He perceived the room he was in from a *slightly* lower vantage point. Objects were a little less clear and a shade dimmer, and the colours had washed out into monochrome. But he was seeing perfectly well *through his nose*!

Rudolph experimented. He blindfolded himself firmly; then he took down a book – and he read it!

He doused the lights. Immediately his nose vision dimmed. Thus it was ordinary light to which his nose was sensitive, not heat as with a rattlesnake.

The Beast was an *organ of vision* – as he had always, in a sense, suspected. Yet due to his custom of keeping it masked with cosmetics, never until now had he known its true potential.

The cherry was a third eye, set in the middle of his face underneath his ordinary eyes.

Perhaps it had only slowly been developing its power all these years under the protective cover of the make-up? And now at last here came the Pauline moment of illumination.

But here was surely a paradox. For in order to make use of his new-found power, it was his *eyes* which he must henceforth hide – while his Beast went naked in the world, something which was against his own deepest principles. His world had abruptly turned upside down. This was indeed the Damascus Road, for Rudolph.

Wouldn't this make of him the very thing which his whole life was tailored to avoid – namely, a visible Beast? Worse still: a blindfolded exhibit on a stage? A sort of Caspar the Counting Horse?

Perhaps. Yet that would be so, only if his ordinary eyes witnessed his shame and disgrace. The eyes are the organs of shame. How often is it said, 'She wouldn't meet my eyes' or 'She averted her eyes'? But his Beast knew no shame. His Beast knew only pride and boldness.

Rudolph's hands itched to put make-up on the Beast as usual. Already it had been nude longer than normal. This was wild and wanton behaviour.

However, he had reached Damascus, and his Beast could see. Now that it had experienced its revelation, it wouldn't ever let him cover it up again.

That night he slept in the raw.

Next morning, he still couldn't cover the Beast. He blindfolded his eyes, instead, and set out to see his domain in a new light.

The July sun was shining brightly, but the world was black and white with shades of grey. Also, it was two-dimensional.

Now, with one eye a person sees the world in two dimensions. With two eyes he sees the world in three dimensions. So with three eyes he should see the world in more dimensions than three! Hastily Rudolph whipped his blindfold off.

There *was* a new depth! He could see that right away. But what was *in* that depth? Something extra, to be sure . . .

Another dimension? Was it, perhaps, *time*? The passage of time itself?

He tried to view the trees as the saplings they had once been. He tried to view their summer foliage fallen off, revealing the bare wooden bones of winter.

The world shuddered like jelly: then it became the same old world again.

Maybe, though he was loathe to admit it, the missing ingredient consisted of other people? A tree leads a very predictable, static life. No hot spots of significance could possibly exist here in this wood. No terrible or wonderful events could colour this landscape, setting up echoes or pre-echoes.

Now, if he were to hold an ancient sword in his hand right now, he felt sure that he would see who had wielded it, and in what panic or blood-lust, and what deaths it had wrought.

He turned. The house itself was steeped in banality, echoing the ordinary days and nights of ordinary people to whom nothing extraordinary had ever happened. Oh, he saw the sheer ordinariness of it now – like an extra coat of paint. A house in the woods supposedly codes for witches, ghosts, incest, village idiots, and lurking horror. There was nothing like that here.

He knew now that his nose-eye must be a very specialized and sensitive detector, for searching out the extraordinary. It was akin to an X-Ray telescope which sees exploding stars where an ordinary telescope only sees dust and darkness. Finding nothing marvellous, though, it only showed him flatness and shades of grey.

Pulling his blindfold back on again, Silvester got into his blue VW (though it was grey at the moment). Steering down the gravel track to the road, he turned east.

Trees everywhere: dull grey trees. He hunted along the ribbon of the road for a glow – a stain – from some past or future accident. It was just a quiet, grey road through a quiet, grey world.

A pick-up truck approached, heading west.

The driver stared in bewildered panic. He must have gone on staring, as the truck wandered right over the crown of the road before correcting. Rudolph slowed, wondering whether this blind-folded expedition was exactly sensible. Yet his Beast said it was okay. His Beast could see perfectly well.

A private road forked off to the right. That was the way in to the estate where defectors lived in their *dachas*, playing endless games of bridge and chess in between being entertained by security-cleared call girls and undergoing debriefing till they were as dry as squeezed lemons.

The Beast observed a faint trail of colour leading up that winding road; and it was of the colour of *strangeness* . . .

Rudolph braked, backed up and twitched his blindfold aside. Now he saw nothing special – except, maybe, a more profound *depth* to that side road. The technicolour of the ordinary world over-whelmed the alien tint.

Resuming his blindfold, he drove slowly up the private road. He wished a Volkswagen had a quieter engine.

Then he passed a sort of tunnel through the forest, caused simply by the alignment of the trunks. *He* wouldn't have noticed it. But his Beast did. Backing up, he stared.

His ordinary eyes only saw a chaos of branches criss-crossing other branches. But the Beast saw right through. It magnified and sharpened what it saw at the end of that tunnel. And that was: a high barbed-wire fence. Beyond that fence, tiny on account of the distance though perfectly clear and enhanced to the eye of his nose, a short stout tree was . . . walking slowly along. He saw it in colour, against the monochrome.

A tree had pulled up its roots to go for a walk. Its two principal branches thrust the other branches out of its way.

Rudolph rubbed his nose in disbelief.

Ah. It must be a guard on patrol. A guard disguised as a tree. It was somebody wearing a bark-coloured camouflage suit and a full-face helmet wreathed with plastic leaves. No doubt the forest was infested with security agents disguised as trees and rocks.

It would have been so much easier to have alsatians set loose in the woods. But perhaps those in charge didn't want the defectors to feel as though they were in a prison camp. Security agencies were given to weird stratagems at times.

His nose didn't agree with this explanation. It insisted on staring.

The 'tree' halted. Its leafy 'helmet' hinged wide open.

A few moments later a fat wood pigeon flew down. Furling its smacking wings against its sides, it threw itself headlong inside the helmet, which snapped shut again.

A *messenger pigeon*, was it? With fresh orders tied to its leg?

There wasn't room for a pigeon *and* a man's head inside the helmet!

Rudolph's ordinary eyes would have rejected what they saw. They wouldn't have seen it at all. But his nose knew what it saw. By now, Rudolph was experiencing tunnel vision: everything about that mobile tree was sharply lit and detailed. Everything else was a dark blur. He had also succumbed to tunnel hearing. He failed to hear the limousine when it purred alongside his Volkswagen.

'That ain't no sweatband, Reuben. It's a goddamn blindfold.'

'So what's he staring at?'

'He can't be staring. Not if he can't see.'

'So how did he drive here, dummy?'

Rudolph snapped out of tunnel vision, and saw two men. One of them was burly and freckle-faced with a mop of red hair, just like a school bully. (There had been no bullies at Rudolph's school, but his mother had taught him to be wary of the type.) The other man was dark, hawk-nosed and muscular, with a square jut of beard like a Pharaoh. This Pharaoh held a pistol.

'Private road, mister. So what's your business?'

The Bully stared into the forest, shading his eyes.

'Can't see nothing. Guess he couldn't either. Maybe he pulled over for a sleep.'

'Don't lead the witness, Craig. I tell you, he was staring. He was rigid. Attentive. *And* he's looking in my face right now, blindfold or no blindfold. He can see through it.'

Rudolph was appalled that his naked Beast was now being inspected at close quarters by someone else, for the first time since he was seven years old. This calamity drove all thought of the walking tree from his head for the moment. If only a laser burst from the Beast would burn these two witnesses down! He clapped a hand to his nose, plunging himself into darkness. With his other hand he tore the blindfold off. Colour vision washed back. The forest was greenly chaotic again.

The Bully named Craig snatched the blindfold from him and pulled it down over his own carroty head. He held a hand in front of his face, fingers wriggling.

'You can't see a *thing* through it.' Craig took it off and tossed it through the open window of the Volkswagen.

'I wear it for my, my, my nose,' stammered Rudolph, overcoming with difficulty a mental block. 'I didn't have time to put my, my, my make-up on.'

'You wear a cloth over your nose? Because you didn't have time to powder it? Christ Almighty.'

'Well, wouldn't *you*? If you had a nose like mine?' Rudolph felt as if he was betraying the Beast.

'Move your hand off your nose. Slowly.'

The Bully stared at the Beast. He guffawed.

'You call *that* something odd? Boy, you've seen nothing. Nothing!'

Nothing should demean the powers of his Beast.

'I just saw a tree going for a walk in the woods!' blurted Rudolph.

'Did you now?'

'It swallowed a pigeon. Whole.'

'Did it now?'

'So that's what you were . . . No, wait a minute. How the hell *were* you . . . *staring*, with your eyes blindfolded?'

Rudolph kept silent.

'Okay, so put that blindfold back on.

'On your *eyes*, dammit.'

As soon as Rudolph adjusted the black cloth, the Pharaoh threw a violent punch full at the Beast. Instinctively Rudolph jerked back. But the punch would never have connected. The Pharaoh had pulled his punch.

The Pharaoh grinned.

'You can see through your *nose*, can't you?'

Miserably, Rudolph nodded.

The Bully's reaction to this confession was quite peculiar. He merely shrugged at his partner.

'So what else is new?'

'Right,' said the Pharaoh. 'Here's what we'll do. I'll escort him to the Farm. You follow on, Craig.' The Pharaoh walked around the Volkswagen and climbed in the passenger door.

'Drive on, Rudolph. You may as well keep the blindfold on. I believe you.'

'But . . . how do you know my name?'

The Pharaoh stared at Rudolph.

'Oh . . . *shit*, that's *unbelievable*!' He rocked with laughter.

Chapter 16

Argus, who lived in mythic times, possessed a hundred eyes. At any one time fifty of these eyes were always wide open. Thus he was constantly looking around himself in all directions. Eventually an enemy lulled him to sleep by playing a flute, and cut his head off. After this, his hundred eyes were scattered upon the tails of peacocks. (There were several peacocks strutting and screaming on the Farm.)

But really, all these old forces of nature – the Gods and demi-Gods and heroes – had never died. They had only been playing possum all the while, hiding out disguised as the pattern on peacocks' tails or whatever, waiting to spring back to life in new form.

Rogers Junior had fallen asleep as Rudolph Red-Nose. But he awoke, all Beast. And his true name was Argus Who Sees All . . .

Awakening, he could see all four walls of the changing room at once. His whole body *saw*: his toes, his ears, his lips, his nipples, his shoulders, his penis – every part of him saw, with a fly's eye sphere of vision. He possessed total skin vision; or at least so it seemed during those first few dizzy all-encompassing moments.

To think that such a partial, pathetic creature as Rudolph had been proud of himself! To think that Rudolph had believed his Beast was a secret power in the world, when his Beast had been little better than an embryo!

The truth about his skin vision was rather more subtle, as Argus soon discovered. Certain areas of his body were quite blind: such as the soles of his feet, his armpits, his groin, and the cheeks of his buttocks (and just as well, too). The areas of full sensitivity (of which there were obviously exactly one hundred) faded off across boundary zones of lesser sensitivity into these blind spots. But the hundred different visual fields all overlapped. The visual effect was total.

He arose, disoriented, swamped by sights. It would all take a little getting used to.

Indeed, he might well have gone insane with the sensory overload. For it was obvious that he couldn't close this body-eye of his. There was no eyelid to shutter it. He feared that his brain might begin erasing unnecessary details – reducing, for instance, the nap on a towel to a plain white sheet, or combining all the hairs on the Japanese doctor's head into a smooth black cap. (Whilst outside this building, his brain would fuse all the billion blades of grass in a meadow into a solid wash of green, locking him into a *cartoon* world . . .)

Wisely, Argus called out for a pitch-black cloak; and one was soon brought to him.

Clasping it about him, he thus shut the majority of his body-eyes.

Yet the changing room at once became dull and tiny. This was like peering into the depths of a cave through a little peephole. It was like trying to view the sky from the bottom of a mine shaft. Sheer deprivation.

The alternative was too demanding, as yet.

'Is that better?' asked Dr Ohira.

Argus hugged the cloak about him, wishing that he could throw the damned thing off, and be his whole self. He felt as incapacitated as a bloodhound with its nose blocked up with wax, or a two-legged spider.

He shook his head.

'You can't switch this thing on and off like a light bulb . . .'

Then he shook his head again, because he had made an interesting discovery. When an ordinary mortal shakes his head, his eyeballs lock on, and track the thing which he's watching. Otherwise the field of vision would swing wildly from side to side. Yet though Argus's ears and lips and nose could all still see, the room hadn't rocked from side to side when he shook his head. Like the computer it was, his rewired brain must be able to compensate for any yawing or pitching of the body.

'This thing, being?' enquired the doctor.

'Vision! Total vision – all about me! My whole body is a compound eye. I can shut my ordinary eyes, but that does nothing. It's like having your eyelids cut off.'

'Ah . . . So you need to go out by night. We have several fine shady temples to shelter you during the fullness of the day.'

'No! I'm *not* nocturnal. I'm a beast of light. I didn't become this, to live my life in darkness and sleep by day. What I need to do is let the natural daylight seep slowly over me. I have to undergo my own dawn of the body in the morning, and my own dusk in the evening. That way, I'll adjust.'

'A new biorhythm, *né*? Please do accept my apologies for this bright room. We will fit dimmer-switches in future. But we couldn't know the nature of your change in advance, could we? You're all unique, so far. And the changed population is up to nineteen individuals, by now. I expect there'll be convergent types as the population climbs.'

'Nineteen of us?'

'We have three changing rooms fully functioning. And Ariel still wants us to speed things up.' Ohira inclined his head. 'If it would cause you distress to leave here prematurely, perhaps I could spend the day examining you? I'll order infra-red lights brought here. You fascinate me, Rudolph.'

'So I should. And the name's Argus.'

'Ah . . . the *Panoptes* of Greek myth. A well-chosen name.'

'But, Ohira-*sensei*,' began Shiba.

Craig McKinnon rapped sharply on the window of the observation room, and frowned.

'Our priorities are altered, *sensei*,' Shiba reminded Ohira.

'Equally, the wishes of our guests are paramount.'

Shiba stepped forward.

'Our task is to get new talents started as quickly as possible. Yours, Argus, will be to explore your own particular talent. This isn't a mere experiment. Something to write a report about. It's a new order of existence. We too will change, as soon as convenient.'

'I can foresee problems of administration,' said Ohira.

'Ariel is considering this, in council with the other changed people.'

'True.'

An impasse seemed to have arisen between the scholar of change, and the man of action. Yet the new Argus knew which side he was on in this dispute. The former Rudolph had been a scholar of the Beast for far too long. Argus was impatient.

From being a loner for so many years, he knew now, too, that he needed many people. A hundred eyes required at least a hundred interesting people to keep an eye on. A hundred? No, thousands. And perhaps with his unique vision he could *see* how to bring this about . . .

Could he? He could see all around himself. But how distantly could he see? How deep into *time*?

Impatience welled in him, mixed with frustration at not being able to throw off his cloak at once. He was in the position of a deep-sea diver coming up to a surface of bright light. He could only do so in slow stages, or else he would burst. Really, it was better if such a diver could sleep *en route*. His awakening here in the changing room was somehow premature.

If his nose had once known what to do, now his whole body knew.

'I want you to put me back to sleep, doctor. I'd like you to transfer me to one of those temples you mention. You will leave the cloak with me – but don't wrap it round me. Lie me on top of it.'

Argus had spoken. Ohira nodded obediently. While Shiba beamed.

Chapter 17

As the first hint of dawn seeped through the temple windows, the hundred eyes of his body awoke him. The visible patches of sky were turning into oyster flesh – studded not with pearls but with star-diamonds, which slowly sank back into the flesh as the valves of day opened wider.

Argus arose from the black cloak, which he found to be draped over a chaise longue. Discovering a stone pitcher of sweet milk and some chicken drumsticks to hand, he breakfasted ravenously. Unfortunately the chicken flesh lacked taste, as though he had a bad cold.

To the eye of his upper lip, as he drank, the pitcher was a great dim cave from which a white flood poured.

Setting down the pitcher, he pushed open the bronze door. Briefly, the door was as high as a skyscraper, to the eyes of his fingertips. Still clutching a drumstick the size of an ostrich leg, he stepped out through a massively pillared portico.

A dozen grey marble steps led down to a violet grassy plain which swept downhill between stands of sycamore and pine. The further it receded from him, the wider swelled the plain. The brightening light was already slowly colour-shifting the grass through blue towards green – and perspective, as he had known it during all his previous life, was plainly out of date . . .

For the eyes of his body did not see by the old rules. For him, now, there was no single point of view – but a hundred viewpoints. There was the viewpoint of his lip, and the viewpoint of a nipple. There was the viewpoint of his penis, and the viewpoint of a finger. And each eye magnified or diminished the view depending on its personal perspective. In some cases 'reverse perspective' even applied: lines seemed to separate, not converge with distance. So he was no longer a single observer standing at one focal point of the world. He felt himself to be diffused through the scene, no longer forced to select one interpretation out of a miriad possibilities. And yet all these alternatives comprised one vision, one multiple vision in his mind: the Many in One.

He was Marcel Duchamp's Nude Descending a Staircase – namely, those temple steps – yet in a far richer sense. For whereas that notorious Dadaist nude had simply been a composite of events in sequence, a time-lapse of bodily motion as perceived by a single witness, what Argus now experienced was all possible dimensions of the world packed into his spherical visual space. Even without moving a pace to left or right, he was able to peer behind the trunks of distant trees, or look around the back of the Ionic temple, or gaze down upon its roof with its six triumphal statues guarding the pediments, front and rear.

He gathered in all light: reflected light, scattered light, and also *earlier* light which had imprinted its photons in the scene the day before or the year before.

It only took a dance-step of the mind to glance around an object to inspect its backside, or – by a different dance-step – to see its circumstances in the past.

In addition, he could far-see. Faintly at present, but all this time the light was increasing. By applying a kind of dance-yoga – certain limb postures – he was sure he would be able to focus on what was far away, beyond the bend of the horizon.

He was like a radio set, receiving not radio waves but bounced light.

He could even, he decided, become invisible – supposing that he chose to cloak himself, not in pitch-black cloth, but in the reflected light of the landscape itself. He should with practice be able to don the trees and grass as a skin of light. Then he would be the Cheshire Cat, emerging out of the camouflage of the visual background, fading away again . . . not into a grin, but into two normal eyes and a patchwork of other parts of his body which had no mastery of light: his insteps, his armpits, his groin and hairy scalp. Nobody seeing him in that camouflage would ever connect him up into a person. Their brains wouldn't let them. Their eyes would only see the scenery reflected in his own hundred skin-eyes.

Soon the last stars were absorbed, and only Venus and Jupiter remained. Argus was conscious, now, of standing at the apex of a great cone of time. All light whatever arrived at his eyes from the immediate or the more distant past. Everything, no matter what, always lay at least a little hindwards in time. And thus, though he could far-see what was happening miles away, he began to understand that he would never be able to *foresee*.

This was troublesome. How had the prototype Argus lost his life? Through lack of foresight. The new Argus might become so dazzled by his perceptions of the past and the present that he failed to notice the *treachery of the future*! Obviously nothing could stab him in the back – for he saw all around himself. Yet a stab might well come from ahead of him in time.

The sun rose in the east: a shimmering yellow dragon-mirror.

A person mustn't stare directly at the risen sun!

How do you turn your gaze away, when you're all eye?

Argus almost ran up the steps back into the temple, to make the thick stone walls his eyelids.

But he stood his ground. He stemmed his panic. It reminded him of the selfsame panic that had surged over him the morning before in the changing room. He had almost . . . *what* had he almost done? He had almost erased all unnecessary details! And this would mean: smoothing a billion blades of grass into a flat green wash, and fusing the ten thousand leaves on a tree into a solid green cloud, and gathering all the streaks and tatters of cloud in the sky into two or three manageable blobs. Like a cartoon. Yes: a cartoon!

Couldn't he transform the sun, and only the sun, into a cartoon of the sun?

Closing his eyes, which of course did nothing to diminish the glare, he *thought* (this hardly does justice to the fierce power of his concentration):

'LET THERE BE NO DIRECT LIGHT!'

'SUN: BE A CARTOON SUN!'

And something . . . shifted.

His body-eyes no longer saw the actual sun. Instead of that blazing luminary, a yellow dish was rising above the horizon, with a polite shine on it, no more. But the rest of the landscape remained aglow with reflected light. Truly, he was a master of seeing! Experimentally, he 'cartooned' some trees, then shifted them back into full leaf.

And then he noticed the tree-man. The tree-man was standing at the far end of the grassy plain, with his back to Argus. As Argus watched telescopically, the tree-man gulped down a fat sparrow.

'Cartooning' the plain, to eliminate its spreading perspective and to cross it more smoothly, Argus trotted down towards the tree-man. He circled round in front of him. A faint, intoxicating perfume drifted from the tree-man's open mouth. In fact, this was the first smell of any sort that Argus had detected since he woke up. Now why was this? It must be because his sense of smell had almost disappeared. No wonder those drumsticks had been tasteless. With so much sensory apparatus tied up with vision, he would never again be able to savour a meal properly, unless he drenched it in chilli sauce and monosodium glutamate. Food had become bland fuel.

Consequently, the fragrance drifting from the tree-man's mouth must be *overwhelming* to anyone else . . .

Blinking at Argus, as though discovered in a breach of etiquette, the tree-man slammed his mouth shut hastily. When he opened it again to speak, the scent had gone.

'Good morning! I'm Silvester.'

'I'm Argus. Who Sees All.'

'Does that include the future too?'

Argus drew back, offended.

'Sorry, my friend! I *do* tend to ask leading questions. This comes from sinking my roots in the soil, and from wearing these Sibylline leaves in my crown. Once I'm permanently rooted, I'll be able to answer all the questions there are. Ambiguously or plainly. I'm an oracle, you see.'

'An oracle? Well, I'm a seer. I see afar, with the eyes of my body.' Argus explained some of his special skills.

'We could make a great team,' he added. He felt a powerful urge to offer himself to Silvester. And this was *most* unusual! It was the first time he had ever felt the slightest urge to offer himself to anyone else, least of all to a tree.

'Yesssss,' sighed Silvester, with the sound of a breeze soughing through branches. 'Yessss . . . a team. The two of us. So different, so . . . complementary. You see; and I foresee. Whatever Ohira thinks, I don't believe we're going to find many physically identical individuals cropping up. I believe we're going to discover *complementary* talents in very different kinds of beings, as diverse as chalk from cheese, as body-eye from bark. We'll bond together, not because we're look-alikes, but so we can fit our talents together. We're like a great jigsaw of many different pieces, of all shapes and sizes. Most of the pieces still haven't been formed.'

'Is that a prophecy – straight from the mouth of the tree?'

Silvester laughed, gurglingly, but he did not answer yea or nay.

'We'll all be symbiotic on one another,' he went on. 'We'll be one single great creature with many specialized talents. Together, we'll be unbeatable. Ariel thought he was going to become a super-man all by himself. But there isn't *room* for this in one person. A human body is already a symbiotic ensemble, did you know? Every single cell in it is a co-operative of separate beings combining for the common good. Now a higher symbiosis is a-dawning – a won-derful collective being! But by ourselves we're still relatively un-specialized . . .'

Argus was indignant.

'Unspecialized! I'm as much of an *Eye* as *you'll* ever see. What do you want: mobile stomachs, walking penises, free-lance lungs?'

'Those are merely organic functions, my friend, not sensory talents.' (Curiously enough, Argus *did* feel intensely friendly towards this tree.) 'What you must realize is that this change is proceeding according to an unconscious *plan*. Now, what is that plan? Well, consider the embryo. It begins as a single cell. Then it divides many times and specializes itself into brain, or limb, or gut tissue or whatever else – according to the genetic plan, and in the correct order. And what do we end up with? With a creature, Man, who is the most unspecialized creature in all the world! Man isn't particularly anything. He lacks the strength of the elephant, or the fleetness of the cheetah, or the eyesight of the falcon. And – would you credit it? – this lack has been the source of Man's greatest success. He can turn his hand to anything at all. He can extend himself in any direction he wants. He uses telescopes to enhance his eyesight, winches to increase his strength, flippers to speed up his swimming. But these tools aren't built into him. So he isn't constrained as the hummingbird is by its bill, or the rhino by its armour plating, or the cheetah by those legs which pretty soon get tired, or the yak by the woolly coat it can never take off.

'And even so, Man has reached a dead end; and of course I include Woman too. He, including She, has become *too* damn general. So he is about to plunge over an evolutionary cliff – like the unfolding embryo itself! – into wonderful new *natural* specialities. The over-specialized, over-complex society of the old-style Normals already mirrors this. The age of Renaissance Man – the epoch of universal man, who embodies all talents within himself, and herself – is over. Ended. Finis.'

Argus scanned the greensward.

'So is Renaissance perspective, over.'

The tree waved a branch to silence him.

'So here is the new plan hatched in the collective unconscious. It's dreamed in our souls, and now the viral drugs lets the body bring it to fruition. So we have Geneva, embodying physical strength. And Ariel, the perfect defence system. And myself: the ability to foresee. And you: the ability to see far. And the others . . .' Silvester spread his woody fingers, to tick them off.

'But look, what's the use of this plan if everybody is separated out like the bits of a dismantled engine?'

'We will have very many specialists.'

'But – '

'But what will bind us all together? Exactly! *That* is the question. Why, the answer to that is that it will be the person, or persons, whose particular speciality is *to join*. The Joiners, in a word. They will link our minds and talents together. They'll channel these to and fro. They'll put them in touch with each other like a telephone exchange. Right now, there still aren't quite enough of us changed people to need the services of a Joiner. Soon there will be. Soon. Remember this! I speak *ex cathedra* now, my watchful friend. I speak as the Oracle.'

Silvester shuffled, withdrawing his roots from the earth. He stamped his feet a few times, to knock the loose soil off them.

'Enough of prophecy for now!'

'Didn't you say you had to be rooted *permanently* before you could be a really genuine oracle?'

'Oh, but I have evidence of these Joiners. A living hint already exists. Behold!' The tree-man pointed.

And Argus beheld.

Chapter 18

Something black skulked from tree to tree along the fringe of the woods, trying to keep out of sight. It was mainly a glossy ebony, with a few honey-coloured patches.

'There's Shetani.'

Argus inspected the creature from all sides, enhancing and magnifying it. What he discerned was a humpy, chameleon-shaped beast the size of a large pig. Its curly tail wound round and round itself like a Catherine wheel. A horny sheath of cartilage hooded its head.

Midway along the humpy back there rode a second, seemingly female creature. She had goggling, lugubrious eyes and an upper lip the size of a tea plate. One of her ears was huge, the other much smaller. She held her thin arms folded in the manner of a praying mantis. Argus realized that the female rider was 'plugged in' to the back of the chameleon-pig by means of a horn on its spine which fitted into the socket of her genitals. Her frail legs flopped astride the flanks of her piggy mount as though paralysed – switched off and de-activated.

What he saw imprinted from the past upon this rider and her mount was that they were not rider and mount at all. They weren't 'they'. But rather, simply 'she'. Puzzled, he tried to see further into the past.

And momentarily he was staring at a black woman with tribal scars high on her cheeks; these scars looked like an extra pair of eyelids, closed. His vision shimmered.

'So what do you make of her?' asked the tree-man.

As though the strange double-being was aware that she was being watched, and spoken about, her body began to mimic patches of leaf-green as a camouflage. But she did not move away.

Argus discovered that he himself had become virtually invisible, as if in sympathy. He had dismembered himself into a loose jigsaw of groin and cranium and other blind parts, afloat upon a background of the greensward. The double-being must be curious about this mimicry of his.

'I call her "The Unit",' said Silvester.

'I can see why. She's one person, divided into two detachable parts, right? The beast-part provides transportation and protection. The human part contains the higher mental functions, and guides the beast.'

'Shetani's a remarkable omen for the way we'll all be plugged into each other one day – through the minds of Joiners. Here, I'll attract her over. She's a bit shy and skittish, but not to worry. Get her on her own, and she's okay. Hold your breath, Argus.'

Silvester opened wide his woody mouth. He vented a gust of intoxicating odour towards the wood. Immediately the chameleon-pig – the beast part of Shetani – raised its snout in the air. With nostrils flaring, it trotted out of cover. But some robins, sparrows, a finch and a nightingale sped ahead of it, like so many feathers being sucked towards a vacuum pump. With a resounding gulp Silvester closed his mouth and belly sphincter, and the birds veered and fled away.

'Shetani!' he coaxed. 'Come on over here. I want to introduce you to my good friend Argus – the Seer. He could see what you were, even before I told him. So you needn't feel shy.'

The chameleon-pig blushed yellow and bilious green. But it continued towards them. The rider slapped the Unit's rump encouragingly with a frail, long-fingered hand.

'It isn't shyness,' piped her voice. Her own body was entirely ebony now. Twenty or so ivory teeth flashed at them. 'It's discretion. To meet a shetani still seems to me like meeting a devil. Even if I'm the shetani, now!'

She pressed her hands down upon the shoulders of the Unit. Thrusting herself upward, she slid her vulva off the nerve-horn. As soon as she began to dismount, her thin legs came back to life to support her. Once on the ground, her stance was crooked. Yet she gave an impression of wiry strength. If she was bent, she was bent like the belly of a bow, straining at an arrow.

Her chameleon-pig wandered off to root about for worms. It licked these up with a long prehensile tongue.

Using his past-sight, Argus saw in flashes: a black girl sitting underneath a spreading mango tree . . . A wizened old man was carving some grotesque blackwood sculpture of a devil-beast. This devil was defecating a baby monster into the mouth of a snake. The old man plied saw and adze and rasp, all made out of scraps from wrecked cars . . .

Next: the girl was running through the ghostly bush by night, pursued by spindly shapes as tall as trees, that reached and plucked at her . . .

Next: dressed in a bright green and orange Java-print cloth which left her shoulders bare, and with cracked rubber sandals on her feet, she was pedalling a wobbling bicycle along a sandy track amidst thorn bushes and gourd trees, whose pendulous fruit hung like long grey sausages. Away to her left she spied a chameleon the size of a cow. Or was it a lion?

Argus relaxed and snapped back to the present.

'So that's what a shetani is. An African bush spirit: I *see*. And now you've become one, eh? Or two. Or one. But you're far from your usual habitat.'

Shetani cocked her large ear, as if to harken to her home thousands of miles away.

'Oh, I was an exchange student. From Mozambique. But I always had dreams, such dreams . . . Then I got mixed up in drugs over here. Acid and coke and other stuff. You see, my Grandad was a carver – '

'Yes, I *do* see.'

'He used dope to set the shetani free from the block of wood. Well, he always *denied* that he used dope. He had to. If he hadn't denied it, and denied the existence of actual spirits, he wouldn't have got his carver's licence or any money from the rural Co-op, would he? I always wanted to be a carver just like him. I *needed* to be. I didn't want to become an agronomist. The trouble was, there was only soft dope over there. Then when I got over here, I disgraced myself . . .'

'But why did you "need" to carve?' Argus thought of looking for himself, but decided this would be impolite.

'Well you see, the shetani *haunted* me. In my dreams they chased me. The only way I could think of to save myself was . . . well, I thought if I carved them in wood that would keep them in their place. Motionless – they wouldn't be able to run after me. But all those drugs I took to do it . . . Well, they were inside me. I mean, the shetani were. The drugs too! So I couldn't carry on studying rural economics. Nuts and pineapples and sisal . . . And I couldn't go back home, either. I had to go sideways, out of sight. If Ariel's man hadn't picked me up, I'd just have rotted, screaming. Now I can separate myself from the dream-beast, can't I? I can ride the dream around. I can *control* it.'

But just then came the warning wail of a siren, from well over a mile distant.

'Probably some idiot, trying to escape their destiny!'

Argus peered at Silvester, as he grumbled, and saw in the past: Frank Caldero pounding along a cinder track between yew hedges, with Ariel gliding overhead like a little pterodactyl . . .

'Well, that's *quite* understandable.' He tapped Silvester consolingly. 'Some people must find the idea takes a bit of getting used to. I mean, *you* hadn't spent your whole life long with a hidden Beast in attendance, eh?'

'It couldn't possibly be The War?' asked Shetani anxiously.

'No, that would be a rising and falling tone,' Silvester reassured her.

Argus focused his body-eyes in the direction of the alert, though by now the siren had cut off. Down at the end of a luminous tunnel, as though on a grainy screen he perceived the watchtower and the steel fence and the locked gateway. Moving the mouth of this visual tunnel, he noticed two rifle-clutching guards sprinting along. Then he overtook two Russian novelists fleeing from the guards. Their manes and hairy coats suggested that they were absconding from Siberia. They fled in a bow-legged, stooping manner with their knuckles nearly brushing the tarmac of the Farm road, just as though they were propelling themselves along with the aid of invisible ski sticks.

He panned about: a Mercedes limousine was lurching off in pursuit, and a helicopter was lifting from the apron near the flag pole . . . Meanwhile, another guard was gesticulating through the locked gate into the wild park beyond. Argus swung his field of view just in time to catch sight of two *more* Russian novelists plunging towards an oak wood. But he couldn't tell their past histories, not while he was employing his far-seeing skill.

'Couple of Neanderthal men are heading for the main road,' he reported. 'Couple more are in the grounds, with us. The gate's still locked, though. So how did they get in?'

'Shinned over it?'

'Impossible!'

'No, from your description those sound very like the super-chimps. *They'd* be able to scale the gate. So . . . now they've broken out. Or rather, now they've broken *in*.'

Argus stared at the gate again.

'Guard seems to have lost the key.'

'Guards aren't allowed in here, except on Ariel's say-so. We're self-governing. But I wonder how pongo got past the alligators?'

'Shall we get over there, and intercept them? Then I'll be able to see how.'

'I can't run. You go ahead, my friend.'

'*I'll* go with you,' volunteered Shetani. Sticking her thin fingers into her toothy mouth, under that vast upper lip, she whistled.

The chameleon-pig raced back to her obediently. Mounting it, she plugged herself in again, and once more her legs hung loose and nerveless. She was the Unit once again, and as such a subtle change came over her expression. Those great goggling eyes looked full of mischief now. She shied. Slapping the rump of her mount, she scampered off.

Argus 'cartooned' the woods, so that he could sprint between the trees more easily. Silvester lumbered along behind, at his own arboreal pace.

Chapter 19

Geneva hustled the two captured superchimps along till they arrived at the Temple of Venus. In fact the metapongids had surrendered to her gladly, as to an old acquaintance. (Though how had they recognized her?) It was merely her disproportionate strength which made them seem hustled, rather than simply led.

Tagging along behind came a goat-hoofed, shaggy-thighed Pan accompanied by a lecherous lesser Satyr, and a water nymph named Nixy. Nixy was the most remarkable of this bunch. An ex-alcoholic kid, who had been on the skids when Ariel's man picked her up, now she was able to breathe underwater in the lakes and rivers of the estate, and she could flap her feet marvellously like flippers and thus pursue and catch fish. She was dressed in a modest leather skirt as a mild bromide to the constant lecherous invitations and voyeurism of the satyr, whose nature it was to be something of a pest. When the satyr acted too rowdily, Pan occasionally thwacked him over the head. And Pan had other uses for him too. This particular Pan was, to Nixy's relief, a homosexual . . .

Ariel was waiting inside the temple at the communications console. Alerted by McKinnon, he had despatched Geneva to apprehend the runaways. This had not taken her very long.

'Here they are!' she bellowed.

Ariel skipped into the doorway and beckoned. He waved Pan and the satyr and Nixy away to their pastimes.

Robina Weber was on the TV screen inside. She had the beginnings of a black eye; and as soon as she caught sight of the two superchimps on her own screen, she signed long and fiercely. The metapongids circled their chests with their palms: 'Honest, we're sorry.' They hid their faces, peeping guiltily through their fingers at the camera mounted above the screen. Robina finally relented and, with a smile, forgave them.

'That's Caesar and Boadicaea you have there, boss. Brutus is on his way back to the compound, under escort. But I'm sorry to say we still haven't caught up with . . . Hang on a minute.' She picked up an orange handset. 'Yes . . . Yes . . .

'Oh Lord, boss, Maccoby just called. He's in the limo at the main gate. Cleo rushed out of the woods with a long branch. She just jumped on the roof of the Merc and vaulted over!'

Ariel flapped about in agitation. The atmosphere crackled with static. Hairs bristled on the superchimps' coats. The two of them backed up against the erotic frescoes, chattering and covering their eyes. 'See no evil.'

'For goodness' sake,' shouted Geneva, 'discharge yourself! You'll do yourself an injury.'

'Yes. Yes. You're right!' Ariel flew to his mighty mistress. She scooped him up in her arms. While Robina stared from the screen, bemused, Geneva groaned and rocked about in ecstasy. Finally, trembling all over, she set Ariel down again. He scuttled back to the console.

'Now listen: send out a search party – use as many people – '

'Maccoby's already on to it.'

'And the helicopter – '

'It's in the air, boss.'

'Cleo *mustn't* get as far as Fairboro, do you hear? So string out a picket line in that direction. And send Jack Nimmo out with the searchers too. Jack's authorized by me personally to tell Cleo that it's high time we made the four metapongids junior citizens in our commonwealth. If she'll just please come back quietly? And he's to remind her that the outside world's full of hoodlums. Okay? *You* stay by the screen. We'll need some interpreting done soon.'

'Is that true about citizenship?' asked Robina. 'Jack and I can't sign untrue statements.'

'I'm not asking you to sign a bloody treaty! I'm just asking you to *tell* them.'

Robina waved her hands.

'Signing *is* how we tell them – obviously! So is it true or not?'

'If they want it that way! Yes, *certainly* they can join us here. Isn't that only fair and just, now that they've forced the issue by escaping?'

While Robina was busy passing on instructions, Ariel confided to Geneva:

'And of course, *now* we have to decide whether that was their purpose. To join the Community of the Changed. If so, they must really have put two and two together.'

'I shouldn't be surprised if they did. Jean Sandwich came away from that compound of theirs with a very strong impression that they know *exactly* what's going on. Robina merely smirked at the notion, need I add?'

'Jack has raised one little point, boss,' said Robina, facing front again. 'Supposing the metapongids all join you, where does that leave Jack and me?'

'You two? Well, it goes without saying that we'll need a couple of interpreters up here. You know, if Caesar and the others aren't to feel alienated. That's assuming they *do* want to live with us. And that means you'll both be able to go through your own change all the sooner, you and Jack. One at a time.'

'We will?' Robina sounded rather more than dubious.

'Really, Robina! You've no *idea* how fulfilling it is, being in on a new cycle of creation. Silvester can vouch for that. The former Mr Caldero. He's really branched out wonderfully, since.'

'Hmm,' said Robina.

'Never mind about that now. Let's get down to business.' Ariel beckoned at the peeping superchimps. 'Now, why did you leave your lovely garden underground?'

Caesar and Boadicaea looked to Robina on the TV screen; Boadicaea signed in reply.

'We want to see your dreams come true,' interpreted Robina.

'That's sweet of you. But in that case, why did Cleo and Brutus rush off in the opposite direction, towards the smelly world?'

'But which way should we go? Which side of which fence? There were hoodlums with guns. So we split up. And we find that this big garden over the fence is another locked place. Maybe it was right to lock us in our garden, if you lock yourselves in yours?'

Caesar signed at Geneva.

'We met *you* in our underground garden. Now you have dreamed a new body for yourself. But I know you. I feel the . . . the congruence (I guess that's the best word) between old-you and new-you. Is the new-you delighted?'

'You can say that again!'

'I signed "very". Try to avoid idioms, huh? Okay: Do you tend this garden? I made out Jean Sandwich was a gardener, remember?'

'I guess it sort of tends itself . . .'

'But there are *hoodlums* outside. Boa again. Over to you, boss.'

'Don't worry about them,' said Ariel. 'Those men keep me secure. We have to have security. The main point is, do you wish to live with us? You can do so, if you want. You'll find lots of trees to climb.'

'That's patronizing and insulting, boss. I won't sign it.'

'Damn it, *I* like climbing trees myself! I glide from bough to bough. Anyway, I *am* a patron. I'm *the* Patron.'

Robina duly signed. And asked in reply:

'If you need the safety of security, are we more safe or less safe, being here?'

Ariel shrugged.

'Six and two-threes.'

'They don't count duodecimally, boss.'

'Just convey the spirit of it, okay?'

Boadicaea scratched her brow thoughtfully before answering.

'We would rather be *less* safe – and learn *more*.'

'Quite! Exactly my sentiment. If I'd wanted to be safe, I'd have stayed in my penthouse forever.'

'We want to learn about your change. Because: if the whole world belongs to you humans at present, and if you all change . . .' Boadicaea trailed off into vague hand-flapping, leaving Robina stranded.

'Ah, you might inherit our ownership? Is that it? No, don't sign that, Robina! Ah, now I see what's in their minds: a new species of superchimps picks up the reins of civilization which we discard, while we changed humans move on to another plane of existence? Ha! Everyone deserves a fantasy! Good thing the poor sods don't know they've been sterilized.'

'They may – just possibly – understand spoken English,' pointed out Geneva.

'Rubbish,' said Robina. 'Look boss, I don't think you need get worried. Superchimps would never want to take over our sort of civilization – no more than dolphins or superdogs would. They're, well, a different species.'

'Amounting to four members.'

'That's three more than you! You people all look like a different species each, boss.'

'We'll get organized. You'll be surprised.'

At that moment a green piggish creature, ridden by an ebony statuette, skidded to a halt in the stone doorway.

'Wheee!' cried the rider. The mount flicked an inordinately long tongue in and out along the floor. 'I've swallowed a snake, I've swallowed a snake!'

Caesar and Boadicaea shrank away in alarm, their hands warding off the menace.

'Shut up, Shetani!' Geneva bawled. 'This isn't the time for games.'

The Unit frolicked away, to be replaced in the doorway by a panting Argus. He gazed at Caesar and Boadicaea.

'So *that's* how you got past the alligators! Nice one. And the electric fence, too! How very ingenious.'

'Ah, welcome, welcome!' called Ariel. 'I'm reliably told that they got out by – '

'I can see how they got out, quite clearly, thank you. As soon as I set eyes on anyone, I see their past history. If I choose.'

'Really? That's *good*. One more success notched up. You must be – ?'

'Argus. Who Sees All. I can see things happening far away, as well.'

'Better still. You can't, by chance, see where Cleopatra is heading for? She's the other pongo who absconded. Last thing I heard, she'd just hopped over the main gate.'

'I'll try.'

Argus departed a little way into the glade. Ariel and Geneva followed him as far as the doorway. With his ordinary eyes tight shut, Argus stared into the sky.

'I spy the main gate . . . That's easy: I already know where it is. Ah, now there's a pick-up truck heading up the highway . . . And the Merc's going in the other direction. Can't see any chimp, though. There's too much damned leaf cover. Now if it was winter –'

'Well, we can't wait till the leaves fall just for you, can we?'

Argus opened his ordinary eyes.

'If I wasn't using far-seeing, I'd easily be able to cartoon all that foliage. Alas, you can't have it both ways. By the way, speaking of winter, what exactly are we all going to do when it turns cold? I can't start wearing clothes. Clothes would blindfold me. And what about that nymph I saw on the way here? Water nymph, right? What happens to her when the water freezes?'

'The winters are quite mild here.'

'Mild enough to go naked?'

'If the weather gets too sharp, there's a huge natural cavern under the high ground. Don't worry, that's all organized. The cavern's fitted out for survival. Though I guess our tree-man and some of the others might prefer to winter in the open air.'

Geneva slapped her robes ebulliently.

'Weather doesn't bother me.'

'Incidentally, Silvester's on the way over. The hedgehog, to my hare! Maybe he'll be able to prophesy where you can find Cleopatra.'

As Argus was walking back towards the temple, Shetani snickered from some bushes. Then she gave vent to an eeerie, blood-curdling howl.

'If you think that'll fool anyone,' shouted Geneva from the doorway, 'you're barking up the wrong tree! Now, get lost! We've got business.'

Inside, the interrogation resumed.

'Now where were we?' asked Ariel. 'Oh yes, do you guys wish to stay here with us, rather than go back to your old quarters? Or did that all get sorted out already? We'll bring Cleo and Brutus here, okay? Cleo, once we've caught up with her and rescued her. We're making a *sweet* world here, you two, not like that smelly one out there. But I give you fair warning: what's here right now will be spreading out *there* pretty soon, and things could get a bit hairy then. If you'll pardon the expression. I dunno, if you were back in your old quarters you might find the transition period less confusing. It's up to you.'

'Phew.' Robina began signing.

'Are you serious?' asked Argus. 'I mean, about changing *everybody*. How do you intend to pull that off?'

'My Japanese doctors are working on it. On some way of dispersing the virus.'

'You mean to spray it from a plane? Or put it in the water supplies? You'd have to hit a lot of sites simultaneously. And abroad too – or else we'll be traced. They'll wipe us out.'

'If you did it either of those ways, Argus, you'd change all the cats and dogs and rats and everything else into the bargain. Supercats? Supermice? Superfleas? That's a no-no.'

Argus stared, but couldn't quite see.

'So you'll have to, what? Dope some product . . . which everyone uses? Such as toothpaste?'

Ariel frowned. His face looked like a shoe, with the laces pulled tight.

'The main problem is unsupervised, *wild* changing. We don't really know what it's like to go through the change without nutrients and sedatives and such. People might hurt, or starve. Shiba thinks it's going to be okay, though. God, when I think of all those poor suppressed people out there leading dull lives in dull bodies! When they could dream, and become their dreams!'

'If they're still conscious during the change, they can't dream.'

'True. Maybe they can hallucinate.'

'And if they *are* conscious, but in agony, maybe they'll change into something monstrous?' said Argus.

'Maybe. Shiba thinks it'll be no worse than prolonged labour pains. That's what the first set of rats really went through: *second childbirth*. We ought to have let them carry on.'

'Yeah, let's look on the bright!' (Indeed, for Argus there were no dark sides any more.) 'Let's give everyone a chance.'

'Yes . . . But there's one small problem called consumer motivation. It would be just fine and dandy if we could hand out bottles labelled "Elixir of Change" to a clamouring populace. Unfortunately we'd promptly have the Government and the God Nuts to contend with.'

'How about setting up your own religious cult in opposition? One with an inner mystery which for once was a physical reality: the communion of the change!'

'That might work, but only if we transferred our whole operation to some place in Africa or South America – somewhere I could practically own. But damn it, man, *this* is my pleasure ground. I decreed it, like Kubla Khan. I'm damned if I'll take off to the Congo or the Mato Grosso!' Ariel shrugged. 'Oh, if only people knew. Once changed, promptly converted, eh? You're typical, Argus. Do you feel the least scrap of regret?'

'Me? I feel like I've been let out of prison after twenty years. I was just a pathetic wretch before.'

'And it'll be the same with everyone, as soon as they've changed. Not *before*, though. If they get wind of this thing in advance, they'll hate it. They'll try to crush it.'

'So they need faith. Like I said.'

'No, *we* need power. We need to put all our powers together. Yours and Silvester's and Shetani's . . . But you've given me the germ of an idea.'

Robina cleared her throat.

'We agree to live with you,' she interpreted. 'But we smell hoodlums.'

'I told you not to worry about those guys!'

'These are *invisible* hoodlums. You do not change in the way we changed. You are the banana plant that bears an apple. We shall stay and smell the difference of the fruit. You can't smell it.'

'What on earth does that mean? Oh, never mind! Robina, when you send Brutus up here, don't forget to include a supply of pongo food. Nuts and bananas and whatnot.'

Argus nudged Ariel.

'Maybe what it means is, being out in these wide open spaces . . . they've gone *ape*?'

A tree shambled, at last, to the doorway and shuffled about there, ill at ease on the smooth stone.

'I foretell trouble,' groaned Silvester, lugubriously.

PART THREE
Thelma

Chapter 20

Argus winked at the others, with his eyes and body-eyes.

'My dear partner, *anybody* can foretell trouble! It's like forecasting the weather. There'll always be a storm somewhere. If there wasn't, there wouldn't be any weather system.'

'Could you possibly be a little more specific?' Ariel asked the tree.

Silvester stamped a few times, thump, thump, thump.

'These chimps have something to do with it,' he said at last. 'We can't assimilate them. They'll be a thorn in our sides.'

'What's this, then? Racialism?'

'*We're* going to be assimilated quite soon. But *they* won't be, hmm, assimilated. I can feel it in my roots.'

'Just what do you mean by being "assimilated"?'

'A Joiner will join us all in a network. That's what I mean. And high time, too!'

'A network of power! I knew it, I knew it!'

Silvester's eyes went blank.

'She who will tie the final knot in the network is a superchimp. Yet then, with their oh so nimble fingers, they'll do their best to untie the network.' Blindly he pointed an accusing branch at Caesar and Boadicaea.

The metapongids screwed their fists against their noses, as if a foul stench was issuing from Silvester's mouth. Since he was in prophetic mood right now, no smell of any kind was issuing from him; so maybe his outstretched branch simply reminded them of a smelly rifle.

'They'll betray us, do you mean?'

'Not *immediately* they won't.'

'Well, *how*?'

Silvester blinked, and looked around puzzled.

'This thing runs deeper than the world itself,' he said. 'Maybe the Joiner will help us understand. I don't.'

'That isn't a whole lot of help. Robina, what's the update?'

'A team's on the way to Fairboro. Should be there any minute. The chopper just lifted off again, with Jack. Shall I patch you through?'

'No, let them concentrate on the task in hand.'

'The superchimps aren't . . . *Godlike*, like us.' Silvester was still struggling with his foresight. 'They're mere mortals.'

'Are we immortal? I wasn't aware of it.'

'Something in us is. Something elemental. Lo, a submerged continent is rising. Only a few peaks are showing at the moment, but what peaks we are! Atlantis lies beneath us: a whole hidden world.' Silvester nodded his crown. '*That's* it.'

'If that's foresight,' said Argus, 'I think I'm better off without it.'

'Maccoby's reached Fairboro, boss,' reported Robina. 'Place seems quiet. He's going to do a U-turn and deploy the picket line back out at . . . Oh shit. They've spotted Cleo. She's there already! She's *in* Fairboro. She just climbed out of the back of a farm truck.'

'Why can't you foresee bloody simple things – *like that*?' cried Ariel, distraught.

By now, Thelma Harvey meekly regretted her decision to retire back to the village of her long-gone girlhood: a period of time when Fairboro had seemed so very much richer in detail.

Had she but realized it earlier, the richness of her memories was directly due to the barrenness of Fairboro. The young Thelma had been obliged, *faute de mieux*, to pay enormous attention, say, to a patch of moss on a stone wall, magnifying it in her imagination into the rain forests of the Amazon . . . Returning to Fairboro in her fifty-fifth year from the boarding school for deaf and dumb children on the outskirts of Pompey, she realized the truth within a very few months. Fairboro wasn't really full of rain forests painted by Douanier Rousseau. The other magical *loci* which she remembered with such nostalgia turned out to be a stagnant pool, a stunted tree and a broken water pump.

However, she did not tune in to the consolations of religion by way of the God Nut radio station broadcasting from Pompey. The notion of being born again in Fairboro struck her as implausible, not to say excessively boisterous. And she had always avoided boisterousness. This was why, with all her faculties about her, she had trained to teach the deaf and dumb. The school had rather resembled a trappist cloister, though without the disadvantages of prayer. Thelma's devotions were paid, instead, to the Romance of the Week Club. She occasionally imagined for herself a mausoleum built out of Romance of the Week selections, all neatly cemented together inside her home as a secret inner wall. When she died, they would remove the outer walls and there it would be: the Mausoleum of Thelma at Fairboro, rivalling Watts Towers and the Tomb of Mausolus at Halicarnassus erected by Queen Artemisia.

Thelma was walking along The Main Street of Fairboro, to pick up her Romance of the Week selection from The Store-cum-Post Office . . .

In meek revenge at the village's betrayal of her memories, Thelma liked to conceive Fairboro entirely in terms of the *Duden Bildwörterbuch*, or pictorial dictionary. Thus she had every single feature of Fairboro listed in her brain in the form of standardized Platonic archetypes, as in the dictionary. So here was The Farm (with The Barn), and here was The Water Tower. There was The Old House, and The Blue House, and The Windmill, and The Derelict House (with The Ghost) . . . Instead of exfoliating every miserable fern into a Carboniferous jungle and every patch of grass into the Pampas – as once she had done – now (with mild vindictiveness) she reduced Fairboro to a schematic. Within this Platonic schematic she was The Spinster, alias The Retired Schoolmistress.

So, as she was walking along The Main Street past The Farm Truck, she noticed the Limousine at the far end of the street, and The Helicopter circling over The Woods . . .

Abruptly, like an eruption of repressed material from her subconscious – like the materialization of Thelma's moth-balled Id itself – a beast-woman coated in thick black fur leapt from the back of the truck, demolishing all blandness at a stroke. This was a creature from before the Stone Age. It was something out of the African Plains three million years BC. She wasn't even a human being. Yet she wasn't an animal – the creature's eyes were too intelligent for that.

Like a priest confronted by a devil, Thelma automatically made signs to the apparition to go away.

And the monster (which she still suspected had sprung from within herself) signed back fluently at Thelma:

'Please help me! Smelly men are chasing me! Don't let them lock me up underground again!'

Immediately various Gothic, and associated, scenarios bloomed in Thelma's mind . . . and withered again (no, this was *not* Mr Rochester's wife!) as she remembered the rumours about the nearby estate.

'Are you from another star?' she signed.

'No, no, no!'

Two strangers were running down The Main Street by now. One of them was waving a rifle.

'Mr Hacker!' shrieked Thelma, in the direction of The Garage.

A burly bearded man in faded blue coveralls crawled from under a tractor. Clutching a heavy spanner, he scrambled to his feet.

Meanwhile Mrs Sandra Glass, who had just that moment ridden her bay gelding around the side of The Blue House, shouted through the open kitchen window for her husband, and urged her mount to a canter. Mr Jim Glass emerged from the kitchen. Picking up an axe from the wood pile, he dashed in Thelma's direction.

'Excuse me,' signed the she-monster hastily. 'I must take you hostage, as in the best movies.'

Thelma squealed and fainted as the she-monster seized hold of her.

She regained her senses high above the ground. She had been carried up the outside ladder to the top of the water tower. Now she was sitting propped upright, with Fairboro spread out before her and twenty-foot depth of water behind. The she-beast huffed and grunted from her efforts.

Realizing that Thelma had recovered consciousness, Mr Hacker tucked the spanner into his coveralls and started up the ladder. Whereupon the she-beast angled Thelma forward threateningly. She screamed.

'Don't, Mr Hacker! I beg you. Go back down! I've been taken *hostage*. She doesn't want to go back with those men!'

'What, that thing speaks English?'

'She understands sign language. So do I.'

One of the strangers below began gabbling quietly into his walkie-talkie.

'Don't panic, ma'am,' called the other. 'Keep quiet, and don't say *anything*. Keep still.'

'Is that thing from a flying saucer, then?' shouted Hacker.

'She says *not*,' Thelma called back.

The helicopter deafened everyone as it sank down on to the open space in front of the tower. The gale from its blades rocked Thelma and her hairy captor to and fro.

A tall blond young man wearing jeans and a Buchanan tartan shirt hopped out of the cabin and ran to the bottom of the ladder. Pulling Mr Hacker out of the way, he ran back a few paces then began signing.

Thelma could easily understand most of what his hands said:

'Please come back with us. (Somebody) promises that you can live with the changed people in the woods, if you wish. (So-and-so) and (So-and-so) are there already. They have chosen a new life. This is very very true. You are in danger from the wild crazy hoodlums here . . .'

'Hey, we aren't wild crazy hoodlums here!' she shouted down at him, signing as she did so to reinforce her message. 'More's the pity,' she thought. But no, that would be boisterous . . .

The blond man looked horribly surprised. He stared at her hands. His own hands jittered.

The she-beast beside her signed:

'I want to see (So-and-so) or (So-and-so) tell me that, on television. We stay up here till then.'

'It'll have to be a video recording!' the blond man bellowed as though somehow this prevented Thelma from eavesdropping on the signs his hands were making at the same time. 'We can't run a cable all the way from the Farm!' One message to her by voice, a different message to the creature by gesture? No: they were the same message. He was simply flustered. 'More flustered,' she thought, 'than me. Despite being kidnapped by my Id.' But no, this creature couldn't really be her Id, not if complete strangers were intent on capturing it . . . She realized that the Mato Grosso and the Jurassic jungles had come to Fairboro at last.

'How long will *that* take?' Thelma called down to him. 'I'm not a pigeon. I can't balance up here all day.'

'Can you please just hold on for half an hour, ma'am? We'll get this all sorted out. Just please don't communicate with the ape. You might get her excited.'

'This is no ape!'

'It is, too! It's a trained ape.'

'Liar!'

The blond man trotted back to the helicopter, to confer with the pilot. The blades whirred again. He waved the helicopter away, then stood anxiously eyeing the top of the water tower . . .

. . . where Thelma was starting to sign questions to her captor – this so-called 'trained ape' – and where her captor was guilelessly replying to them all.

Chapter 21

The helicopter took a whole hour to return; and by then Thelma knew full well, whatever the thrills of the jungle, that she had been ludicrously shamed in the eyes of all her neighbours. For by now, simply *everyone* had gathered.

During the first ten minutes or so of her enforced vigil on top of that water tower, she was still in the eyes of spectators the same old Miss Thelma, plainly in peril of her life from an escaped beast. Yet as the minutes rolled by, and as her bum grew numb and as vertigo assailed her, and as strange emotions climbed up her spine like snakes, she was seen by all to be blatantly cuddling and canoodling with the hairy creature just as if that water tower was lovers' lane at dusk. The small crowd began to view her predicament in a new light, and even to titter and nudge. Miss Thelma was visibly having it off – at long last – in the most blatantly exhibitionist manner. That the beast was a she-beast was by no means obvious from down below. Yet Thelma's own realization of its actual sex was no consolation. When and if her good neighbours discovered, they would laugh themselves into paroxysms, maintaining stoutly that Miss Thelma couldn't tell the difference. Or, more scandalously still, that she *preferred* a distaff lover, just so long as the female was butch and hairy enough. ('Oh, it was a *terrible* thing for the poor dear, but you *must* admit . . .') Thelma's head buzzed with shame.

The twenty-foot depth of water yawning behind her became a well of loneliness. If tongues wagged too much she might be found drowned in it one day. The Water Reservoir would bloat The Corpse, of The Disgraced Spinster.

Yet this was far from being *all* she decided, perched up there on her embarrassing eminence, one hand waggling conversationally while her other hand clutched a hot waist . . .

Trained ape, indeed! She had known that for a lie, the moment the blond man uttered it.

Her captor was called Cleopatra. She had spelled out her name. (Cleopatra's whiskered cheek, and her steamrollered nose and bulging muzzle, were in enforced proximity to Thelma's own cheek. Yet the chimp's mouth did not reek of bacterial plaque, or fermenting bananas. If anything, her breath smelled of peppermint toothpaste.) And Cleopatra had once been an ordinary chimp but she had been changed in mind and body into a creature never seen on Earth before . . .

Yet the experiment didn't end there. The whole reason for it, explained Cleo, was to change not chimps but *human beings*. The aim was to change people into creatures as different from ordinary men and women as Cleo was different from an ordinary chimp. Cleo had only actually seen one such changed human, who had stared down one day into the Chimporium, the chimps' underground prison-garden. But she *knew* there were others. They all knew. It was the only reason for their own change. They had seen enough films to work out that humans always experimented on animals first of all. So she and her friends had escaped – out of overpowering curiosity and from a desire for liberty, equality and metamorphraternity.

Thelma began to dream of a plan which would rescue her from shame, and the prospect of floating bloated in the water tank one day. She could save her face, by changing it . . .

Finally the helicopter did descend. A battery TV set and video cassette recorder were unloaded. The TV screen was aimed up at the top of the tower. The blond man spoke to Mr Hacker, who grumbled, but went and fetched a long pole from his garage.

Thelma thought at first that the blond man was fastening a noose to the end of the pole, in the approved manner of animal catchers. But no: he was attaching a pair of binoculars on a strap. He climbed a little way up the ladder, until he could pass the binoculars up to the changed chimp, then backed down again and switched the TV set on.

Cleo stared through the binoculars at the silent video film, for all the world like some snooty countess in her furs scrutinizing a distant ballet through her lorgnette. On the screen, another changed chimp made signs. But without binoculars, the image was too small for Thelma to see clearly.

'Tsk,' tutted Cleo to herself. 'Tsk, tsk.' Whether these clickings conveyed approval or disgruntlement, or whether Cleo was merely filing the information noisily, the way she might crack a tough nut in her jaws, Thelma couldn't decide.

Cleopatra saw the whole recording through twice.

'Tsk,' she said, and tossed down the binoculars, narrowly missing the blond man.

'Okay,' she signed down at him. 'This hostage is free. I agree. I'm coming down.'

As gallantly as possible, considering their awkward situation, Cleo helped Thelma turn, and plant her feet upon the rungs. She handed her down a way.

Quivering, Thelma descended – and as soon as Thelma was safely on the ground, Cleopatra followed her, fast as a fireman down a greased pole. Mr Hacker moved to support the trembling Thelma, but she shook him off. His approach frankly suggested to her, 'Once dishonoured, free for all.' She was shaking more from cramp than shock, in any case. She hobbled over to the blond man. So that no one else but he and Cleo could understand, she signed to him:

'Listen: I *know* what's going on. Your chimp told me *everything*. You're changing people, not just chimps. And I want to change too! I want sanctuary.'

Seeing the limousine depart with Miss Thelma and the trained ape secluded in the back with curtains drawn, the villagers of Fairboro speculated.

'I always said there was something odd about her – '

'Born and bred here! But when she came back she didn't join in; she just *watched* us all – '

'I say she worked for the Estate all along. They planted her here –

110

what's the word? – like a sleeper. In espionage, you know? Her cover just got blown. Did you see how she talked to that monster with her hands? I bet she never taught at any school in Pompey. I bet she worked in Intelligence. That was no ape, either! It was something made in a test tube – '

'But that's illegal,' Mr Hacker said. 'Monkeying around with the image of God is illegal.'

Jim Glass, still clutching his axe, was by way of employment a salesman of best bull and ram and stallion semen. Thus he felt conflicting emotions at this revelation. His own job involved test tubes, and a certain amount of monkeying around with the image (as yet unsacred) of cow and sheep and stallion. He had a sneaking suspicion that if the God Nuts won the day, cows too might become sacred, as in India.

'Look, there are bound to be secret Government research projects. I'd say we ought to keep out of this, seeing as we don't know what's going on.'

'You don't happen to be a *sleeper* too?' asked Mr Hacker. He patted the spanner in his coverall pocket significantly.

Jim Glass laughed nervously.

'Me? You know me. I only sleep when the sun's down. *I* think we just saw a UFO pilot from another star.'

'Miss Thelma said *not*. Unless she was lying.'

'Or maybe it was from the *future*.'

'The sort of future when we'll all have turned ourselves into apes by monkeying around with our bodies?'

'Well, of course, if a new Ice Age happens . . .'

'You think they're breeding people for a new Ice Age, on the Estate? So what does the Government know, that it isn't telling us? Are the glaciers getting thicker?'

From the back of patient Brandysnap, Sandra Glass chipped in.

'Did you see that movie last week on TV? A dozen people got shot just for asking questions like that about nuclear power stations – and they were all Government employees. That's true to life.'

'If I was living on the edge of a nuclear waste dump, I'd want to know it,' said Mr Hacker fiercely.

'Just as soon as you start sprouting an extra head, I'll believe it,' said Jim Glass.

'No, we ought to report this to somebody.'

'What? Report that Miss Thelma just eloped with a hairy humanoid from the year Three Thousand?'

'Twelve people were murdered, for uncovering a secret. That's true to life.'

'The Reborn Church ought to be interested. They could send investigators.'

'Lord, Hacker, we don't need that mob camping on our doorstep! That's crazy.'

'Nothing crazy about loving God's laws, Mr Glass. Disobeying them is what got the world into its present mess. I want to know what's happening.'

'Let's ask Miss Thelma, soon as she gets back.'

'*If* she gets back.'

'She went of her own free will. They didn't hypnotize her.'

'Oh no? How about all that business of waving fingers in her face?'

'That was sign talk. I saw a feature on TV about – '

'Yeah, like code. Like a *secret* language. Miss Thelma spoke it.'

'Well, she was a deaf and dumb teacher.'

'But *who to*?'

'It's a *nice* life here, Mr Hacker, exactly as it is.' Sandra Glass patted Brandysnap's shoulder. 'It's an oasis.' She began to canter off, but reined in briefly.

'*Nothing* happens here,' she called over her shoulder. 'That's what's nice about it.' And rode on.

Pulling out his spanner, Mr Hacker smacked his palm a few times.

'A helicopter? Armed guards? A monkey-man? Miss Thelma an Intelligence agent? That's *nothing*?' He headed back towards the tractor he was servicing. 'Okay, it's nothing,' he told himself. 'Happens every day. Routine. I'll be damned.'

Chapter 22

'There are snoopers in Fairboro,' Ariel warned Maccoby on the screen. 'They've been driving round our perimeter in a couple of campers, and now they're both parked beside Hacker's Garage. Argus saw them with his special vision.'

'They might be relatives of Hacker's. There's been some trouble in Pompey. Bit of rioting. A few fires.'

'Argus says they look like God Nuts. I believe him.'

'What do you want *me* to do about it? We brought that schoolmistress in. We couldn't have brought the whole damn village! What about the milk collections? What about the school bus? What about the mail? There are just too many damn links with the outside world, sir.'

'One of those links is with God Nuts. Now they're camping out in Fairboro.'

'Let's not worry, sir. I'd say they're a lot more containable than a Government task force would be – hunting for a missing community!'

'It would be fine,' said Silvester, 'if what we were involved in was an alien invasion by weird-looking creatures who could take over the roles and appearances of ordinary men and women. I mean, that's the usual version. The canonical version. But this is the other way round, isn't it? Ordinary folk turn into freaks. As it were. Well, not *freaks* exactly . . . But in the eyes of ordinary mortals – '

'Is this the trouble you foretold?' Geneva asked him. 'The trouble the superchimps would cause?'

Silvester shuffled.

'No. It isn't. I can't really say what the trouble is. I've a sneaking suspicion I *did* say exactly what it was, but I didn't realize so at the time. Darn, it's almost on the tip of . . . something or other.' Silvester shook his crown, and a leaf fell. 'That's the trouble with foretelling. Now listen to me: I am going to foretell something – *ex cathedra* too, me being in a temple right now. Hear this: Fairboro is *no* problem, and as soon as Thelma Harvey wakes up – '

Ariel interrupted.

'She ought to wake up tomorrow. Right, Reuben?'

'She hasn't changed a lot physically, apart from getting to look younger – '

'So it must all have happened in her brain.'

'*Please* don't interrupt a prophecy! Now look what's happened! I've gone and lost that bit of it. What else was there? Ah: this God Nut snooping is definitely to our advantage.'

'I fail to see how.'

'But I'm telling you!' Silvester snapped at Ariel, as though he had just broken a branch. 'If you're determined to change the outside world, you *do not* begin with random mass treatment – '

'Shiba received the first batch of the drug mixed into cans of Diet Pepsi yesterday evening, sir, from our Maxton plant – '

Silvester persevered.

'You begin by converting key individuals to our view of things.'

'Well, *exactly*. That's what I've been thinking of since – '

'So the God Nuts are the ideal target. They've infiltrated politics and the economy. They've got further in the military than *you* suppose. As for the media – '

Ariel held up a little hand. It crackled bluely.

'This isn't prophecy.'

Silvester's eyes became a glassy green, as though sap was about to burst from his eyeballs.

'And now they have come to you! Of their own accord!'

'Oh . . . I see . . .'

'You will take over the inner circle of the God Nut movement. You will pick these snoopers up, Ariel, and hold them. I *prophesy* that soon we shall have a shape-mimic among us – who shall be named Prote. And we shall have a mind-mimic, whose name shall be Mentamorpha! They're completing their change *right now*.'

Silvester's eyes cleared. Remembering his own prophecy, he shivered, setting all his leaves a-rustle.

'Is Thelma Harvey going to be a mind-mimic?'

But Silvester was speechless.

'More likely it's that transvestite, sex-change guy,' observed Maccoby helpfully, 'or else that out-of-work actress. They're both due out tomorrow.'

'Damn good idea about using those snoopers for infiltration, though. Good prophecy, Silvester. But I think, Reuben, we'd best wait to see if Silvester's right about our new talents before we pick the snoopers up.'

'Should I send out a small surveillance team?'

'That's *quite* unnecessary,' Argus said haughtily. 'I can easily keep an eye on them. Leaving ninety-nine to spare.'

'Shiba might want to try the virus on the God Nuts, cold turkey style,' suggested Maccoby. 'With no other drugs. He thinks the brain probably provides its own opiates. After all, *they* came and bothered us. Not us, them.' He sounded hopeful of some agony dealt to Ariel's enemies.

'No-o-o-o,' said Silvester, hollowly.

'No to brain opiates? No to cold turkey?'

'We don't want a *rogue changer* amongst us, Ariel.'

'In what way, rogue?'

Silvester blinked.

'I can't say.'

'You've got twenty beds now?' Ariel asked Maccoby.

'Full field hospital, sir. Incidentally, as soon as Thelma Harvey is discharged she'll be able to interpret for the Pongos, won't she? So we can accept either Jack or Robina, if you still need a minimum of two interpreters. Jack seems pretty enthusiastic about changing, by all accounts.'

'We need two, yes. Silvester raised some doubts about the superchimps.'

'So that's solved by Miss Harvey. I'll slot Jack in, then Robina later. I'm just trying to keep our schedule balanced, if we have to go on using intravenous and sedatives.'

'You're doing a fine job, Reuben. I'm just sorry you'll have to put off your own change for so long.'

'Well, that's security for you. But don't worry. I can wait.'

Although his roots were on stony ground, Silvester had drifted into a semi-trance state.

'*Robina the Rogue* . . .' he said loudly.

'What?' cried Ariel. 'She isn't with us a hundred per cent? Where is she, anyway?'

Argus went out to stare up at the sky.

'With the chimps,' he called. 'She's in the Rotondo, up by the heath. Busy signing to the gang. Shame I can't read hands.'

'Trouble, trouble,' gurgled Silvester.

'Yes – but *what sort*?'

'I can't *quite* – '

'You're a useless prophet. Useless!'

Silvester opened his eyes.

'There's gratitude for you,' he sighed. 'And I just told you what you'd do about the God Nuts.'

'Okay, sorry. You were very useful. Even though I'd have thought of it myself, in another few minutes. I'd have had to, wouldn't I? Otherwise you couldn't have prophesied it.'

The Rotondo rose from the edge of the high heath. A volcano might have dripped there (though it hadn't): around slabs and boulders like gobs of cooled lava flowed purple rivers of heather and sulphurous waves of gorse. Glossy stands of rhododendron circled this upland, their green dams cupping the sun-toasted air.

Set on a ridge between the hot heath and the coolly-leafed descent, the Rotondo was a boldly rounded dome supported on eight stout shafts. Functionally it suggested a hooded salver on legs, for serving a giant turkey or perhaps a roast roc – in stone instead of silver. A circular bench occupied the paved base; around this sprawled the superchimps like feasting Romans, devouring a picnic of bananas, mincemeat tarts, cashew nuts and cold frankfurters. Robina paced about the circle, signing. Jack Nimmo was nowhere near.

To Argus's distant eyes the party looked like a conspiracy. Four senators were lounging in hairy robes, planning a *coup d'état*, to be led by that matronly female Cassius whose hair, on fire, was the torch of their sedition . . .

Chapter 23

'Why, I never was *alive* before!'

This realization filled Thelma with wonder and admiration as, unabashed, she inspected her naked limbs. Though her figure was still reedy, she felt altogether more sprightly, and her skin was fresh again. She twitched her body experimentally, sending signals racing to her fingers and toes.

The Japanese doctor clucked deferentially. She ignored him for the moment. He wasn't *quite* alive; nor was that other face peering through the observation window. ('Oh yes, I got a whole room to

116

myself, didn't I? Not just a bed in the big tent.') It didn't matter if they saw her naked.

Beyond, in the hospital marquee, she could sense peers of hers who were coming slowly alive, but who slept on for a little while longer . . .

Alive! For the past fifty-five years all she had been was a Normality Machine: a machine for filtering out the extraordinary, so that she never even noticed it.

'That's why people generally forget their dreams,' she said to herself. 'That's why they can't see a wonder if it slaps them in the face. They're Normality Machines.'

Now she knew *exactly* what dreams were. They were nothing less than the dump, the pit and cesspool into which the Normality Machine offloaded all the wonders that couldn't be seen, all the thoughts that were unthinkable, all the inaccessible emotions. Every day a net was dragged ahead of you, scooping all these wonderful, absurd and marvellous things up in advance, then dumping them down the drain at night. Dreams were the emptying of the Normality Nets. You got to watch the cataract – since the machine couldn't arrange everything . . . then it vanished and got forgotten.

Some people must have a few holes in their nets, though. This sort of person saw visions and dreamed while wide awake. But the neighbouring machines would do their darnedest to knit the holes together supportively, using the knitting needles of militant normality.

Perhaps she had been slightly unfair to the Japanese doctor? Had he not invented an acid for eating away the net? But his own net still remained in position . . . scooping ahead, dumping.

What else did this net do? Why, *it held you together*. It stopped you from leaking into other people. It kept you together as a 'person' with a certain fixed body shape and a fixed turn of mind.

The net was a sort of *Duden* dictionary. It re-arranged and labelled everything in the blandest way: as The Leg, The Tree, The Man, The House. Yet there were other orders of existence entirely! The net excluded them. Every night it flushed them away down into darkness.

Out on the estate, at the moment, she sensed many other people whose normality nets had been rotted away. She leaked towards those wonderful, changed people. She sent signals speeding out to those others 'toes' and 'fingers' of hers. This was how she felt related to them. She received signals back, and wove these together on the loom of her hands and feet.

For a moment she saw with the hundred eyes of Argus. (He was her right-hand index finger.) She discharged electricity with Ariel, who was gliding – this was his first real Jovian lightning bolt. (And he was her left-hand index finger.) She sprinted through a dappled glade. (Geneva was the big toe of her left foot.) She rooted into the soil (Silvester was the big toe of her right foot), and sensed futurity in the flow lines of the planet's skin . . .

With a polite bow, Ohira drew her attention to the matter of costume. He had laid out three alternatives, should she wish to wear clothes. There was a white Ancient Roman *palla*, a silver jumpsuit, and her own former blouse and skirt, brown and cream as a cup of coffee. That would do. She pulled on the blouse and skirt, but she ignored the bra. Her breasts were firmer now. She selected sneakers for her feet.

She beamed at the doctor, forgiving him for his ordinariness.

'You'll be specially interested in the people who wake up this morning!'

'Really? Do you weigh up probabilities? Without direct access to the data?'

'Without access? I can monitor everyone in my network, doctor.'

'Remarkable. Your network consists of – ?'

'Every changed person, so far. They're all a part of my body. They extend my body in all directions. That's why my own body didn't need any special change, itself.'

'Other than certain, shall we say, cosmetic improvements?'

'True. But I'm no flighty fool. I'm still plain. Renewed, but plain. That's good enough for me.' She wagged a finger at Ohira. 'I have a whole extra body right here. And here. And here. Each finger and each toe *connects me*. They put me in touch.'

'Ah so? I wonder, would you lose touch with part of your network if I were to, well, inject one of those fingers with local anaesthetic?'

'I've no idea!'

'I'd rather appreciate it, Miss . . .' began Ohira.

'Thelma! My body's still plain old Thelma. I see no reason to change my name.'

Just then Maccoby bustled in from the observation room, without knocking.

'Would you describe yourself as a sort of puppeteer, then?' he asked, without preamble. 'A puppet operator? Can you "move" Ariel and the others against their will?'

'What a finely tuned security machine you are, Reuben!'

'How do you know my first name? I don't recall – '

'*Ariel* knows it.'

'You read minds?' asked Ohira hopefully.

'No, it isn't like that. It's more like . . . well, imagine there's a physicist or a musician in my network. Now, *I* don't know an M from a C squared. Or a flat from a sharp. But suppose I was to stand up in front of a blackboard, or sit at a concert grand. The equations and the music would just flow out of me, like second nature. And third nature, and fourth nature, and many other natures! I'm a switchboard. I just bring us together, like one extended body in lots of different places. Muscle here, farsight over there, electric spark somewhere else. All the parts are individuals, though.

'Of course,' she added lightly, 'given your own privileged position as – shall we say? – Ariel's right hand, you may feel a little bit jealous. I advise you not to feel that way, Reuben. Don't be over-ambitious – except for change.'

She reached out her left hand, with her index finger sticking out. She seemed not so much to be pointing at Maccoby as to be offering him a mystic handclasp. Puzzled, Maccoby stretched out his own hand.

'Ow!' he yelped.

'There is a little of Ariel's sting, Reuben. And Argus is keeping an eye on you.'

'Me, I wasn't up to anything,' blustered Maccoby.

'Of course not. Just remember: Ariel hasn't abdicated. No throne is vacant.'

Thus, with a flick of her ferule, did Thelma put the chief of security in his place. For perhaps he would like to over-reach himself . . .

'I'm a hundred per cent loyal! But how about *you*, Miss Thelma?

That was what had me bothered. You were saying you could twist Mr Ariel round your little finger.'

'Does a body rebel against itself? Does the heart declare war on the lungs?' Thelma switched her attention to Ohira. 'Now, doctor, I wish to be present when Mentamorpha and Prote wake up.'

'Who are they?'

'I'll show you. Then I'll escort them up to the Temple of Venus to meet the others. Later on, Ariel will want *you*, Reuben, to take a team into Fairboro to bring back the God Nut spies. I'll give you a note, too, for Mrs Sandra Glass, inviting her up here for a little visit. You'll find her at the Blue House. I really *do* fancy her for a Centaur. She spends that much time in the saddle, she might as well be fused to the body of a horse.'

'Isn't she married? Hasn't she got any kids?'

'Oh, I suppose so! How banal. Yes: there's Jim Glass, and a boy and a girl.'

'Well, aren't they going to miss her? I mean, we don't want Fairboro full of missing persons.'

'Really, Reuben, a place simply cannot be *full* of missing persons.'

'You know what I mean, Miss Thelma. We oughtn't to recruit so close to home. It isn't safe.'

'Phooey. Those people are in a dreamless sleep. Just as I was. They'd hardly notice.'

'Somebody isn't asleep. Somebody tipped off the God Nuts. The evidence seems to point to that garage man, Hacker.'

'You'd best fetch him in too, hadn't you?' Thelma thought a moment. 'Oh, all right: him, *instead* of Sandra Glass.'

'Sure, that's easy. People have seen those mysterious visitors at his place. Now the visitors disappear, and so does he. But what about his wife?'

'His wife? He's a widower. Now, if *that's* all settled, Mentamorpha and Prote really *are* just about to wake up. I want to be there.'

The ring finger of her left hand and the corresponding finger of her right hand – neither of which had ever worn rings – were tingling now, in tandem with two corresponding toes.

Which, she realized, would make her class register complete.

She totted them all up. Ten finger-persons, and ten toe-persons, yes. In addition, if she plucked a chord of two strings (as it were) then this manoeuvre yielded a further ten changed people, linked to her on a duo-digital basis: left finger, left toe; right finger, right toe. Then there were ten more linked on a cross-over pairing: right to left, left to right. Total: forty. With the next two awakenings, her tribe was definitely full up.

She couldn't have a centaur in her tribe after all. Pity.

But changes were going on all the time. Even now, several more changes were on the way. So, quite soon, there would have to be another Joiner such as Thelma. And then another and another. Would they all be linked in turn by a kind of President? A sort of Olympian Zeus?

'It's a new type of clan system,' decided Thelma. 'Each tribe is a colony of individuals. Like a sponge or a coral. Massed together, we'll form the reef on which the seas of the world will break in vain!

'But I'm not the chief of my tribe. I'm more like the head dress that a chief wears. Consisting of exactly forty feathers.

'So who *does* wear the head dress? I don't – because I *am* the head dress. Ariel doesn't wear it, either. He's one of the feathers. Maybe nobody wears it. Sponges and corals don't have big chiefs.'

Chapter 24

Two days later, soon after breakfast time, Ariel received word at the Temple of Venus that the God Nut snoopers had been captured quietly in a pre-dawn raid on Hacker's garage. There were six spies in all. Three males were segregated in one camper with three females sleeping in the other. Surprised in their bunks, they had been tranquillized, trussed up and driven back in their own vehicles to the Farm – along with Mr Hacker, snatched from his bed.

As soon as Ariel learnt this, he concentrated his thoughts strongly on Thelma; and presently she arrived in person, from the nearby Gothic Temple.

Thelma's new home pleased her mightily. With its turrets and gables which yielded a romantic silhouette from every possible angle; with its circular gallery underneath a traceried dome; with its enigmatic archways leading into *trompe l'oeil* halls – these were actually small anterooms equipped with camp beds and a few toilet essentials – the Gothic Temple might have sprung quintessentially from the finest Romance of the Week offering stacked in her clapboard house in Fairboro . . .

She arrived together with Mentamorpha and Prote. Prote's special talent was to alter his appearance quite quickly to imitate any other human being, though preferably a female. Mentamorpha's was to imitate the *mind* of anybody. She could read all their memories, make use of all their skills, and behave exactly as they would have behaved.

For the moment, Prote had copied the guise of Thelma. Thus, in effect, *two* Thelmas arrived at the temple. But one could tell them apart on careful inspection, since only the real Thelma behaved exactly as Thelma should. Prote's gestures, facial expressions and turns of phrase exposed him, ultimately, as a superficial copy.

Mentamorpha had mimicked Thelma too – but psychologically. Or, more exactly, what she had mimicked was the *substratum* of Thelma's personality and memories from before the time the viral drug expanded her horizons. (Mentamorpha couldn't mimic the new, expanded Thelma because this would have necessarily included a mental homunculus of Mentamorpha herself, thus leading to the well-known logical problem of infinite regress . . .) Consequently, Mentamorpha was behaving in a shamed, confused and spinsterly way as though, after years of chaste sublimation, she had just been publicly raped by an ape. This abashed demeanour conflicted, rather, with her own body image. For Mentamorpha was a glamorous peroxide blonde with bobbed hair, a pert turned-up nose, sultry lips and noteworthy bosoms. It was this body which had derailed her career as an actress; no one would cast her in any but the most blatant roles.

So, in a sense, *three* Thelmas arrived at the temple. One of them was real. One of them looked the part. And one of them acted it – at least according to the previous script. Thelma-prime, whose view of the world was larger and more courageous now, sincerely hoped that her two temporary twins – the Look-Alike one, and the Think-Alike one – would be able to function effectively as a team.

Ariel offered everyone orange juice.

'Can't have those God Nuts visiting up here. Goes without saying.

One look at Shetani or Silvester, and they'd foam at the mouth. So we'll all have to go down there for the interrogation. And the – I hope – impersonation. Dear Geneva will guard us, just in case they burst their bonds.'

'We can't let them see you, either,' Thelma pointed out. 'Wouldn't you rather stay up here?'

'No, I wouldn't. But I'll keep out of sight, behind mirror-glass.'

Ariel toasted them in orange juice.

'Here's to Change. And here's confusion to the God Nuts!'

They clinked tumblers and drank. Though, judging by the look on Mentamorpha-Thelma's face, she feared the orange juice was secretly spiked with gin . . .

It was a misty morning as the five changed people travelled down through the glades and across the meadows, with Ariel riding up on Geneva's shoulder. When they emerged at last from the mists into the path of a small searchlight shining from the watchtower to mark their course, it looked to the guards on high as though a double-image of Thelma was striding out of the cottony blur – accompanied by an additional out-of-the-body personality, which had settled in frigid, ghostly transparency over an otherwise lovable blonde. The sight of Mentamorpha particularly confused them. She was bewitching – yet bewitched. She was captivating, yet held captive – somehow by herself.

Mr Hacker had already begun his change, which would at the very least change his mind about things. Should he still be able to pass muster as an ordinary fellow afterwards – should he not become physically bizarre – he might even be able to return to his garage, as Ariel's agent in Fairboro. How he had howled at being parted from it!

The God Nuts, however, needed investigating first . . .

By the time Ariel's party arrived at the ranch house, McKinnon and Maccoby between them had already discovered who was the leader of each of the two trios, male and female. (Or, in God Nut jargon, who was the Parent of each Trinity.) So far they had found out little else. The two 'parents' were already handcuffed to heavy Burmese teak chairs in the interview room, when four of the changed people filed in. (While Ariel slipped by another route into a cubby hole behind the mirror.)

The male parent was a short, stocky, black-bearded fellow with wild watery blue eyes. His cropped black hair was balding at the crown, thus giving the impression of a monkish tonsure. He was still wearing the striped blue pyjamas he had had on in his bunk in the camper; but in this setting the pyjamas looked more like a convict suit.

The female parent was a grossly overweight young woman. Her chins quivered in a cascade. Her green eyes were squeezed cunningly inside caves by the buttocks of her cheeks. Her long brown hair, greasily unwashed, fell in tangled rats' tails down an all-enveloping brown woollen nightdress.

Both parents' feet were bare, and Geneva observed karate calluses on the man's, while the woman's feet were dropsical soft clubs – sandbags with thick ingrowing claws. Both of the God Nuts wore stainless steel crosses around their necks on thin chains.

The fat young woman stared at the giantess in disgusted envy at her muscular magnificence. While, in turn, the convict-monk stared at Mentamorpha – who was doing her brittle modesty trick. He stared with a stunned, avaunting lust which her exuberant prudishness both redirected and inflamed to new strength. Both pairs of God Nut eyes flicked hastily away to the two Look-Alike Thelmas. From the knowing nods exchanged by the God Nuts, obviously they presumed these Thelmas to be cloned duplicates, making a monkey of natural procreation.

'This isn't any Government place, is it?' the convict-monk asked roughly, as though *he* was conducting the interrogation. Rather than the other way about. 'It's *private*, right? It's all part of King Enterprises, who are really rich cats! Think they're above *God's Law*! But I tell you: there's only one *King*, the *King* of *Heaven*!'

Though he didn't realize it, the man was busily interrogating himself.

'The Holy Family know where we are. You can't escape the eyes of the *Righteous Rangers*.'

He spoke like a printed tract for simpletons, with many emphases all over the place . . .

'You hear this: *riches* don't protect nobody from *Righteousness*! God made Man in his own *image*. And Man shall not remake that image to suit his own whim or *pleasure*. Nor shall he xerox that image

124

in multiple copies, creating the like of robot *courtesans* – because God didn't make Men like unto *ants*. Out of untampered loins alone comes life with a *soul*.'

He glared at the two Thelma Look-Alikes. Though really, Mentamorpha much more closely resembled a courtesan, for all the psychological chastity armour in which she was arrayed.

Thelma gestured to her Look-Alike. With a sly grin, Prote began shifting his shape.

Now, Prote *did* prefer the female form. But the fat woman's similarity to a hippo presented massive problems. Prote would have ended up with very spongy flesh and fat, and a lot of air inside his tissues. To copy the male parent, the easier model, Prote only had to grow somewhat denser . . .

For a time – during which the convict-monk ranted on in a way very reminiscent of an old-style preacher who meant to talk the sand out of an hour-glass, then stand the glass on its head and talk the sand out again for another hour – the speaker found nothing to stem his flow. His audience stood about in contented silence.

Presently, though, 'Thelma's' hair had turned black and balding. Her eyes had taken on a watery blue hue. A thick morning stubble was sprouting from . . . *his* chin.

Slack-jawed, the convict-monk shut up. And just at the very moment that he did shut up, the alluring Mentamorpha cast off the corset of spinsterly cobwebs – and carried on his rant for him in a sweet and silky voice, devilishly at odds with the words themselves:

'. . . a test tube is *no tool* of Procreation! I say, *shatter* those glass tools!' She pouted. '*Enough* of this drivel. Ah'm Harry Fullerton, reborn in the *bosom* of the Lord. I guess the Lord only has one bosom, unlike me. Ah'm leading Christ's Commando Unit – the People's Police of *Purity* – to spy out this nest of snakes. And ah'm to report direct to the *righteous* Regional Apostle himself, in Pompey. He's Reverend Drew Hayes, of *course*, and Reverend Hayes is one of the Twelve Apostles of the new Conclave of Christ in this whole blessèd nation, with his home HQ *sacredly* protected by seven God-fearing Guardians and ee-lec-tronics – '

'Shaddup!' howled Fullerton, wrenching at his handcuffs.

Sweetly Mentamorpha continued:

'Reverend Drew's unlisted phone number is: prefix – '

Prote looked the perfect convict-monk already. Yet he still continued improving in minor ways upon his beard and build, adding nuances.

'Witchcraft!' shrieked the fat woman. She began to pound her doughy feet upon the floor . . .

Before too long, Ariel in his cubby hole had an entire master plan roughed out. By crooking the appropriate finger every now and then, Thelma became privy to it as it unfolded.

By now Prote was the absolute spit'n' image of Harry Fullerton, God Nut. In this guise Prote would penetrate the guarded inner sanctum of Reverend Drew Hayes. In private audience, Prote and Mentamorpha would hold Hayes at gun-point while respectively they copied his body and picked his mind. Then the false Harry Fullerton would take over the role of Drew Hayes, with his new blonde secretary to prompt him. The real Drew Hayes would be chloroformed and crated up or rolled in a carpet, and carried out – on the new Reverend's orders – to a waiting McKinnon to be whisked back to the Farm for conversion. Meanwhile . . .

They all heard shouting, somewhere else in the ranch house. A gun cracked.

Immediately the real Harry Fullerton began crying out, 'We're here! We're here! Save our Souls!'

Geneva quieted him by clamping his lips together between finger and thumb. The fat girl promptly took up the cry. Reaching out, Geneva silenced her similarly. But what an awkward, splayed stance this was; Geneva couldn't move.

'Let 'em squawk,' ordered Thelma. 'Bring Ariel in here, then guard the door.'

There was renewed outcry from the captives as Geneva dashed out, to return moments later bearing Ariel. She slammed the door and jammed the heavy teak chair with the fat woman in it underneath the handle. As soon as Harry Fullerton saw the winged sprite perched on the shoulder of the Amazon, he began bleating in panic; the fat woman whinnied asthmatically. For Ariel was visibly a devil from out of the Hell of their minds.

'Quiet!' Ariel commanded.

Neither God Nut paid the least attention. Ariel flapped down to the floor, therefore, stretched out a finger and shocked Fullerton senseless. Hopping around, he piped at the fat woman:

'I don't want to give the lady a shock! Even if her brains *are* scrambled eggs! But I will. I will!'

The fat woman gawped, but from now on she merely mumbled prayers.

The group waited.

And they waited.

'What the devil's going on?' asked Ariel, eventually.

'I've been trying to get Argus to focus on it,' Thelma said. 'But he can't see through walls.'

Someone pounded on the door.

('Sir! Sir!')

Geneva humped the bulk of the chair and God Nut woman out of the way. Outside the door panted Craig McKinnon.

'The apes, sir. Robina Weber. They came out of the maze – '

'Ah!'

'In the west wing now. Collared Ohira.'

'Ohira? But they mustn't harm *him*!'

'He's okay. Co-operating.'

'But what do they *want*?'

'Can of Diet Pepsi. They want a can of – '

'*What*? You don't have to shoot the place up to get a drink around here! Room service isn't that goddamn slack, even in the woods – '

'*Special* can, sir. Drugged one. They made Ohira open the safe.'

'Oh, I *see*. No dammit, I don't. Robina only had to ask. She can go ahead with her change any time she wants.'

McKinnon had recovered his wind by now.

'I guess she's hoping to smuggle a can out for analysis, sir. They demanded transport too. They want one of the campers the God Nuts were using.'

'Robina, a God Nut? Rubbish! And the superchimps *can't* be God Nuts – what's in it for them? So what do they want transport for? Has Cleo learnt nothing from the last trip to Fairboro?'

'I can ask them,' volunteered Thelma. 'Remember: I can handle sign language.'

'Yes! Yes! But what's it all *about*? I should have listened to Silvester – if only he'd been making more sense.'

'Those damned pongos must have watched too many hostage movies in Miss Weber's compound,' suggested McKinnon, 'during their, er, formative period.'

'Hoodlums!' Ariel spluttered. '*They* complain about hoodlums? *They're* the goddamn hoodlums hereabouts. Let's get over there.'

'Brutus has a hand gun,' McKinnon warned. 'He's keeping it jammed up against Ohira's skull.'

Ariel groaned like an assassinated Caesar.

'Oh the brute! Never mind. Come on.'

Geneva scooped him up.

When they arrived, the four metapongids, Robina and their prisoner were still in Ariel's former study. This was a walnut-panelled room with French windows, through which the rebels were about to exit to the camper. The vehicle had now been brought up, with all reasonable delay, and parked – though not too close.

Walnut bookcases were crowded with journals about genetics, evolutionary theory, pharmacology and medicine. A massive painting (heavily framed in Grinling Gibbons style) of a band of cavemen waylaying a mammoth was hinged out from the wall, disclosing an open safe. Inside, the safe looked more like a fridge, as it was entirely given over to dozens of stacked cans of Diet Pepsi. Each of these had been injected with the virus through a pinprick puncture, which was then soldered shut, retaining the carbonation. Mahogany desk and rosewood harpsichord by the window were loaded with thriving house plants. There were Wandering Jews and bromeliads, ivies and ferns, a Japanese fan palm . . .

Geneva heaved a great sigh.

'Oh my, oh my: all my plants – I forgot all about you! Frank, I mean Silvester, *said* he'd bring you all here. And I forgot!'

Then Geneva noticed the Mother-in-Law's Tongue thrusting its green and yellow blades up from the lid of the harpsichord. The *Sansevieria* had been watered, dusted and misted. Its swords were glossier, sharper and more malicious than ever.

Robina, meanwhile, stood clutching a single unopened can of Diet Pepsi – a terrorist with a Molotov cocktail. Ohira was babbling something suicidally apologetic in Japanese. Thelma started signing across the room to Cleopatra – who semaphored back: 'Apples on banana plant!' Robina called out, 'I have to do this, boss. I have to change with all my wits about me – away from all of you!'

But Geneva, with a roar, launched herself across the room towards her vegetable enemy on the harpsichord. Misinterpreting her sudden rush, Caesar snatched up the first object to hand to ward her off; and this proved to be the *Sansevieria* in its pot . . .

Geneva ran directly into the blades of the plant.

Now truly, a person – least of all a giantess – cannot quite be stabbed to death by a Mother-in-Law's Tongue, even of the 'De fer' variety, no matter how skilfully or haphazardly it is wielded. Spiky as those 'De fer' swords are, they still possess a certain flexibility.

Yet two of the points pricked through her robe into the muscle of her belly. With a cry of agony Geneva staggered back, gripping the blades which had wounded her. She crashed mightily to her knees, still clutching those swords as though she meant to fall upon them in a Roman suicide – or as though these were magic swords which, once stuck into the stone of her flesh, could never be withdrawn.

'Oh Mother Josie!' she wailed. 'Only this could have killed me! Only this! And in the womb, too.

'Oh Ariel,' she called mournfully. 'I am dying, Ariel, dying.'

'What nonsense!' sniffed Thelma.

But Ariel, heedless alike of his own skin, and of his scheme to transform the human race into metahumanity, scuttled towards his Amazon's side.

'Geneva, my love,' he squeaked.

And Craig McKinnon leapt to tackle him and protect his master's body with his own.

As Ariel jumped on to Geneva's bowed shoulders, to boost delirious joy into the pleasure centres of her brain through electrical induction, McKinnon crashed into her in what was now a scrummage – and groaned aloud with the backwash of ecstasy.

'Oh love-death,' moaned Geneva. 'Delirium of being pierced.'

'Live, live,' sang Ariel. 'Live and love. Be healed.'

In the midst of this confusion, Robina and the superchimp quartet slipped quietly out of the French windows, dragging Ohira with them to the waiting camper . . .

PART FOUR
Robina

Chapter 25

Some two weeks later, many of the changed gathered on the scuffed lawn between the Palladian quadrants of the Temple of Venus for the latest progress report from Ariel.

Presently he appeared, riding on Geneva's shoulder. Geneva had quite recovered her spirits after her wounding by *Sansevieria* (indeed she had done so within the hour) but a rent remained in her robe which she refused to let Ariel, with his defter fingers, sew up. The frayed edge of that rent bore the slight stain of her own dried blood.

By this date Ariel's audience included a considerable number of newly changed persons who were outside of Thelma's network, and not yet in one of their own.

Amongst these was Phaethon, who could wreathe himself in flames. In a reverse of the usual yogic progress over beds of hot charcoal, Phaethon left charred footsteps where he trod. Silvester had shunned him in horror from the first time he flamed on, fearing a conflagration.

There was Icara, a light-boned child of a woman with great butterfly wings sprouting from her spine. These wings were black on the outside, vermilion within. She could flutter aloft from a standing start, not simply glide in the style of a flying fox like Ariel.

And there were others who were equally remarkable in one way or another, visibly or not so visibly. Two of the most noteworthy new talents had already hurriedly been seconded off the estate to Salvation Heights in Pompey, to assist the pioneer infiltrators Prote and Mentamorpha, even though the new recruits weren't linked in Thelma's network.

'We've done *rather* well so far,' announced Ariel modestly, from on high. 'Reverend Drew Hayes, most fanatical of the God Nut Apostles, has been smuggled back to us. The contents of his files have been transferred into our own computer. So now we have all the dope we need on God Nut sympathizers in key public posts in this part of the country. That's over two hundred prime Nuts to roast with the change, by and by.

'Hayes is going through his own change very nicely – while Fred Fantazios and Foobert are doing sterling work backing up our two impersonators in the heart of Hayes' HQ. Fred Fantazios, as many of you know from his brief stay here, can adopt the form of any inanimate object. Whether it would be a boulder or a motorbike or even a pond, that's what the beholder sees and feels. So currently Fred is masquerading as a leather armchair over at Salvation Heights. Or is he an eagle lectern, with a big Bible on it? I forget. While Foobert, who specializes in animals, is for his part guarding our brave team in the guise of a Doberman Pinscher – a new acquisition of "Apostle Hayes" which usefully happens to keep his other righteous guardians at bay.

'But where is Robina Weber? And where are the metapongids? They haven't gone to the authorities. If they had, we would have been staked out by investigators by now. They just dropped Ohira by the roadside, and vanished with that camper. So where are they, Argus? Eh?'

Obediently Argus surveyed the four quarters of the sky, hunting for any leakage of light from the absconders.

The stretched turquoise silk overhead was brushed with a white calligraphy of clouds: drifting, indecipherable poems in *ts'ao shu* grass-writing style. Below, the morning was excessively drenched in green-on-green. Argus hastily cartooned the trees around the clearing, the better to peer through them at more light-bouncing sky. He had found that he could cartoon what was *close* at hand, while he was far-seeing.

'I'm blind to them. That's it: they're in my blind spot. It's like . . . when I do *this*.'

Argus faded into the green background for a while. Only aspects of him remained visible. Of these scattered aspects of a person – hair, two eyes, a groin – the onlookers could make little sense.

'Something's *hiding* them from me,' came his disembodied voice. Then Argus returned from the greenery.

Ariel called for Silvester, who stumped forward.

'Well, you were right about the superchimps. So what can you foretell about them now?'

'It's on the tip of my . . . whatever it is. But it won't come. I'm like Argus. He has his blind spot – I have my dumb spot.'

'*Try!*'

Silvester dug his roots into the ground. His eyes went blank. As though straining in a mighty wind, he shuddered. And he spoke.

'Rumpelstiltskin stamps his foot right through the floor, when his real name is spoken. What is underneath the floor? *We are.* His foot sticks through the floor like a hernia. It's a rupture in the intestines of the other world. Robina and her chimps are hiding behind the hernia. *We* are the hernia. She'll try to patch the hernia up for Rumpelstiltskin. When she does, then I'll be the tree underneath the hill, my crown below the ground. Rumpelstiltskin is only the *alias* of God. That isn't his real name . . .'

Silvester opened his eyes, and sighed.

'You see, it's all nonsense.'

Thelma crooked the big toe of her right foot, to put herself in touch with Silvester. Next, she summoned the eyes of Argus. Then she joined the whole jigsaw of her tribe together (apart from Prote and Mentamorpha, far away, who mustn't be disturbed) . . .

Forty feathers (minus two) were gathered in a head-dress. Number one was a peacock-blue feather with a hundred eyes upon it. Number two was blue with electricity. Number three was piebald, ebony and clay . . .

And *she* was the binding of the head-dress.

Yet what face peered out from the feathers? *What head wore it?*

With her hundred eyes, and other talents, she strove to see . . .

'Hey!' called Phaethon hoarsely. His flames flickered feebly for attention. Charred footprints disfigured the whole sward. They looped this way and that in and around the tribe or Thelma, as though he had been dancing a fire dance to attract their notice. Icara and others had taken refuge inside the temple or amongst the trees. From these they stared out as from a cave mouth of from foliage at the first Promethean event in history. Or perhaps at something even more unusual . . .

All of a sudden Thelma's whole tribe were jostling about, stretching their limbs. Clamour arose.

'Where've you *been*?' demanded Phaethon.

'Been?' asked Thelma, puzzled. 'We've been here. I mean, we *are* here. What do you mean?'

'You've been playing statues for the best part of an hour! You haven't moved an inch!' Phaethon pointed at the sun for confirmation; and sure enough the sun had skipped onward in the sky, nearer noon. Shadows had sidestepped a couple of paces.

'But I was . . . trying to see,' said Thelma. 'I was trying to, yes, see what's hiding Robina and the superchimps. No, that isn't it! Now I remember. I was trying to see *the face*: the face in the head-dress. Our tribe is like a head-dress of forty feathers, Phaethon . . .'

'So what did you see?'

To that, the answer was nothing: nothing at all. Thelma looked at the sun again. It was obvious from where it now stood that she and her whole tribe had just passed through a period of blank unconsciousness – a period so blank that it seemed to occupy no time at all. And during that pause of time, she realized, they had *been* the Face: the hidden Face, staring out.

As soon as Thelma understood this, and communicated it, Shetani took fright. She scampered off, squealing, into the woods while her rider tried in vain to control herself.

Standing upright on Geneva's shoulder, Ariel called for order.

Chapter 26

At first light, Robina arose with a groan. Her joints ached. Her flesh sweated. Her nerves were hot wires. It was the worst hangover she had ever endured, and all from a single can of Diet Pepsi, drunk many days earlier.

Though the camper had been home to one feverish human and four metapongids for days on end, it was still relatively tidy. For the superchimps had methodically been dumping all the litter and mostly they had ignored the chemical toilet in favour of retiring behind bushes, except when it was raining. When the weather was dry, too, Caesar and Boadicaea and Brutus had preferred to make a sleeping nest outside leaving Cleo to watch over the often delirious Robina.

The vehicle was parked in an overgrown, disused stone quarry thirty miles from the Farm. The nearest hamlet was Stenton, eight miles away. Uprooted saplings and shrubs camouflaged the roof of the camper. But tonight these would have to be removed – wouldn't they? Robina tried to remember what the four super-chimps had decided the night before. Yes, tonight she was to sleep rough in a nest with Caesar and Cleo. Boadicaea would drive the camper to the outskirts of Stenton to steal some food, while Brutus rode shotgun, armed with the pistol. The larder was almost bare.

Could Boadicaea drive?

Robina seemed to recall giving Boadicaea a few driving lessons soon after they arrived at their camp . . .

Her belly growled. Gas shifted in her guts, uttering a long tuba note. Overnight her intestines had become a convoluted, self-playing wind instrument. Hot golden tubes of brass . . .

Her bladder felt fit to burst, and thirst was burning her throat. Hearing Robina beginning to blunder about, Cleo awoke, scrambled up and steadied the woman.

Robina let herself be led outside, first to relieve herself and be wiped with a bunch of leaves, then to be guided through a brake of elder bushes to where a spring trickled down the rockface into a cool clear pond. Cleo cupped up water with her hands. When Robina had slaked her thirst, Cleo undressed the woman and bathed her, then dried her on the towel of her own warm fur.

Cleo carefully examined the woman's body in the gathering daylight, searching for any noteworthy physical changes. Finding none, she dressed Robina again.

'I'm hungry,' signed Robina. If the tuba wasn't soon stuffed with some food to mute it, it would play some disgusting oompahs . . .

The others were up and about when they returned to the camper. Inside the vehicle, Caesar was setting out breakfast for Robina, consisting of the last scrapings of the larder: a foil tray of cold cannelloni, a bar of fudge and a packet of dried apricots.

'What are you eating?' signed Robina, though she was ravenous.

'We find roots and worms and beetles and fungi.'

Robina protested feebly.

'It's okay as a diet. We aren't fussy. Eat,' Caesar ordered her.

Quickly Robina packed her groaning entrails with the pasta, fruit and fudge.

'Later, we feed you fungi if they smell okay. But better, I think, that we gather human food *last* night. Sorry! We aren't used to organizing picnics.'

'You're doing fine. You're very kind.'

'Our pleasure. Boa and Brutus go to fetch food tonight, when it's dark. Not before. If people see a monkey at the steering wheel, they have a fit.'

So it *was* true; she had taught one of the superchimps to drive . . .

Later, the troupe set out on foot to forage.

Cleopatra led Robina gently by the hand. They made their way through the tangled defiles of the quarry, and up onto a rumpled, coarse grassland bounded by a low swell of bushy hills.

The wind whispered softly. They started a rabbit, and Caesar threw a stone, but missed. Brutus pointed the pistol. Doubting his aim, he did not fire. Boadicaea picked clover and chewed the sweet flower heads.

A hawk hovered high, ahead. Robina stared at it. The hawk was actually . . . a vulture. They were a band of apemen, just newly *erectus*, out gathering and hunting. What Brutus held in his hand was a flint axehead.

Robina's fever had abated somewhat. Now she knew exactly where she was. And when. Thus, hand in hand with her ancient ancestor, she stumbled on into the dawn of time.

She heard the sulky roaring of a lion beyond the hill . . .

And the humming of fat bumble-bees . . .

Caesar swatted one bee between his fists, popped it into his mouth and crunched it up.

The grass sang, *swish-swish,* and the sun glared down upon a rolling savannah. A contrail bubbling out of a high-flying spark of silver seemed a queer intrusion from a different time-zone.

The lion was standing silhouetted on the skyline. Clutching Cleopatra's fur, Robina pointed.

'Lion!'

'Calm yourself. There's no lion up there. There's nothing.'

'Lion!' Robina broke away from her attendant and started searching for a stick or stone.

Cleopatra ambled along with her, sympathetically.

'You're feverish. There's only us, Robina.'

'No! There's something else.'

Was that really a lion, out there on this ancient African plain? Robina shaded her eyes, to mask the glare of the palaeohuman sun.

The lion stood up on its hind legs and strolled down from the crest of the hill towards the foragers. He was a lion-man. With his tawny skin, his great lion's mane and face, and his long twitching tail, he was a golden king.

As though she had fallen even further into the past, Robina for a moment saw a flesh-eating dinosaur walking down towards her, swinging its great hips.

Brutus had found an ants' nest. Busily he stirred it with the pistol and sucked the clambering ants off the barrel. Caesar noticed some fungi, and began sniffing them.

Now the intruder was a harlequin man: a naked pied piper of all humanity. The left side of his naked body was black. The right side was white. He sported flaming red hair. Breasts stood out from his chest. A thousand expressions and physiognomies flickered across his face in succession.

Boadicaea chattered an alarm call. At once, all four metapongids were up on tiptoes staring in the direction of the naked harlequin, though not directly at it. Their hairs bristled. They made warding-off signs. Brutus waved the pistol around.

'Something *is* here,' Cleopatra gestured. 'You're right. I feel it. My skin creeps. But it isn't *completely* here. What is it? I'll tell you: it's the apple on the banana plant! It's the strangeness we felt about the changing of the humans!'

The harlequin halted among the superchimps, though none of them saw it. The being's face was less legion now. The different faces which composed its countenance, in dizzyingly rapid sequence, were those of Ariel, Geneva, Shetani, Argus . . .

The harlequin took Robina by the hand, and led her away from the metapongids, some distance across the huge savannah. Somewhere a rhinoceros grunted. Up on the hillside an elephant was tusk-wrestling a tree, trying to force it to the ground. Around her innumerable dark-skinned hominids milled and danced in lines. These hominids passed right through her, and she through them. They were ghosts, echoes of an earlier existence. Would this be her special talent: to detect echoes of all previous eras – rather as Argus could detect trapped light, past photographs of any person?

'Robina,' the patchwork being said, 'you've just got to help me out.'

'Help *you* out? It's *me* who's hallucinating!'

Curiously, Robina did not feel afraid. It seemed as though the harlequin was draining her fear away; draining away, at the same time, her fear of madness . . .

Now the harlequin wore the faces of Silvester, Pan and Nixy.

'No, you aren't hallucinating. This is the Past you are seeing. It is the *other* Past.'

'Other . . . past? But surely there's only one past?'

The brown-skinned people were erecting a city on the plain. None of the houses had any doors, but only open archways. Sometimes people paused to copulate openly in the streets. It was a city without any interest in privacy.

'Actually, Robina, there would appear to be *two* Pasts. Two branches from the same stem, two trunks from the same root. Oh, I'd begun to suspect this over the past ten thousand years or so! But I let things ride. I don't know that I had much choice in the matter. Maybe it even amused me! Maybe I thought I'd learn something more about myself. And now look at the fix I'm in!'

A nomad invasion swept across the plain. This forced the brown people of the city to invent weapons and tactics, and to build a city wall with massive gates. Yet though many heroes died in the skirmishes outside those gates, though there was blood and fear and pain, also there was a curious sense of ballet, or game, about the unfolding war. This history was a chess game played with living knights and pawns.

Weapons clashed around her. Some of the protagonists were altering their bodily shapes to those of beasts and monsters. They became demons, marvels with wild talents, wild emotions embodied in flesh and bone, in claw and feather. She saw griffins and ogres, harpies, angels and centaurs. These pranced and flew and trampled till Beauty and Good had defeated Evil and Ugliness, for the time being at any rate. Robina saw nothing in the city resembling a temple, church or shrine. No prayers were offered up, no sacrifices . . .

'You've been nuts on God for such ages! Yet you never worked out what a God is. Always on the lookout for something supernatural!' The harlequin sighed. 'I don't suppose I can blame you. I only made the connection, myself, in the last three thousand years.'

'Are you saying you *know* what God is? But I don't think I believe in God.'

'A very commendable attitude. But, baby, I *am* God. At least, I'm part of God. And God is *you*. Yes, you: the whole damn lot of you! You, as you *might* have been. But were not.

'Now you listen to me, Robina Weber. Hear this: there were *two* possible paths for the evolution of higher intelligence on this world. One was your own path – which was the construction of a personal self, sustained by the reality-machines of your separate minds. And there was *our* path: the path of collective awareness, arising from the empathy of the primal horde.

'*That latter* is God. Once it has a chance to grow, and play games with itself, and learn. God is the human mind raised to the power of the whole human race. Its evolution leads to Godly powers. It brings command over our own bodies, and command over our minds, linked in the Overself.'

The city had become steel and glass. What looked like alien beings rubbed shoulders with the human inhabitants. Yet they were all, Robina sensed, from the same root stock. The 'aliens' were weirdly mutated not by genetic trial and error, but by willed intention.

Outside the city, rested a silver space vehicle in the shape of an egg. It was the size of a baseball stadium. Plainly this vehicle wasn't propelled by rockets. Control of gravity, or of the continuum itself, must power it. Hovercraft with transparent domes were bearing alien beings to board it. Strange air writhed in these domes, poisonous fumes. Mythological beings supervised the loading.

'We're sending part of ourself away from the Earth,' the harlequin commented. 'We want to see whether we will split over interstellar distances like an amoeba, thus giving birth to ourself once more. It's an experiment.

'We may discover other alien Gods like ourself out there already. It wouldn't surprise us. Perhaps we'll learn how to unite with them in

Godly marriage. Perhaps a conflict game will develop; maybe *that* will be a better way to learn and grow. Sometimes I think that the universe is one big game. Some future version of me is playing the game with myself. In a sense, I may still be a child-God . . .

'And when the game has been played out, when at last I understand the universe, I can start it off all over again with a few changes in the rules . . .

'*But* . . . It seems the universe is a bit stranger than this. Though I've been suspecting it for a while. And that brings me back to you, Robina.'

The harlequin grimaced. Its face was all the faces of the first tribe of the Farm, in turn.

'You can't be God,' said Robina. 'Not if you don't know everything!'

'I'm the next best thing, my dear. Nearer – my God! – than thee. And the true name of this God is *Pansapiens* . . .

'Pansapiens evolved naturally in our time-stream. Alas, either the universe or I myself would seem to have given rise to an echo, to a mirror reality where I didn't arise at all. Shall we call that echo the Path of Self? It seems to balance the Other Path – just as an antimatter cosmos may balance the matter cosmos. It's a sort of particle pair production, if you're fond of Physics . . .

'There's resonance between these two streams, Robina. Because of this resonance, you people on the Path of Self have called up aspects of me, time and again. Not that it ever interfered with me directly, before! But all your gallery of supernatural beings has obviously leached out of my own reality. All your devils and angels and Olympian Gods and mythical beasts – and your whole *concept* of a Deity! – come from me. Though never in any substantial, demonstrable way. Until now . . .

'I've had this dreamlike – or maybe I ought to say *nightmare*-like – awareness of your time-stream. But I thought it was unreal. A sort of "maybe"-reality. An unborn Siamese twin. And all this while the twin has been growing up alongside me, walking that other path, leaching on me unawares. Even worshipping me! What a weird double universe this is, after all!'

'So *we* are your . . . nightmare! Is that what we are?'

'That's a *wee* bit harsh on you. I simply don't *belong* over here, do you see? Pansapiens didn't evolve in this time-stream. Individual *selves* evolved.

'Now the reality-machine has broken down, for the People of the Change. And I'm leaking through. My powers are leaking through. But the People of the Change don't know me directly. How could they? I am them collectively, but at a much higher level. Anyway, they're still patterned into many separate selves – even if they do form tribes, in imitation of the ur-hordes I evolved out of. This could *split* my being, Robina. But not in the way I planned it – not as a grand venture to the stars. Splitting back here at home will pull rags and tatters off me. It'll make me a schizophrenic. Oh, senseless things will happen! And all because it isn't your natural path.'

'But couldn't it be our natural path from here on?'

'No! Because you have to be what you are; and that is: *selves*. *I* don't want to be lots of selves. This creature talking to you right now is a separated self.

'Listen to me. You're going to become a Joiner, like Thelma. You'll be the Joiner of the next mini-horde. But it's all useless! The rules of the Path of Self are written indelibly in you. It takes *aeons* to evolve into a proper God. Whole ages spent playing the life game. With you people there'll just be chaos. Prodigality. Arbitrariness. Rococo artifice. Caprice. You can see how eccentric the changes are already! You've tapped the *mature* powers of Pansapiens – that's the power to change yourselves at will – because you've short-circuited your reality machine with that goddamn virus drug of yours. That's what it really does in your case: it forms a bridgehead to Pansapiens. How can that be your future, Robina, when it never was your past? Oh, you might well have been echoing me for millennia with all your religions and your myths. But those are *not* your real selves.

'You'll have to patch this rupture, my dear. If you don't, there'll be a mess.'

'But the chimps changed into perfectly acceptable superchimps! They haven't turned out a mess.'

'Different strokes for different folks, Robina! They're okay, because there isn't any resonance between them and me. And there isn't any Pan-pongo time-stream. Not unless you've started one now, with your meddling.'

'But how could we? The chimps have all been neutered.'

'Don't ask *me* how! I'm merely a God. And something of an *enfant-Dieu* into the bargain, I suspect! I'm not an expert in multiple realities. Oh, I can handle higher dimensions in the abstract well enough to design a star-drive – but that's beside the point. The point is that all this changing has got to stop.'

'But this could be your big challenge. If you could come to terms with the people who've always worshipped you, you could show us so much. How to build a starship, for example!'

'Will you *please* listen to me? To come to terms with you, as you put it, *you* would have to lose your selves in *me*. How does that grab you, after several million years of constructing personal selves? Pretty senseless, huh? Waste of time? And it's worse, from my point of view. If the Path of Self really does balance my own Collective Path in some higher equation I don't know about, well, by fusing the two I'd become . . .'

'Unbalanced?'

'Loony? You said it, not me. I don't mind if you people worship me from a discreet distance. I don't even mind it if the occasional individual picks up "miraculous" traits of mine now and again. But getting myself incarnated in you *en masse* as a series of squabbling tribal Godlets is definitely *not on*. You aren't Pansapiens, nor were meant to be. Loony, indeed? I'd be back in my infantile, many-tribes stage. I'd be thrust back to the time before I got properly organized. It would be like having my mind split in a kaleidoscope. And all the time you would have access to my mature powers.'

'Well, I'll believe you . . . Yet you can't tell Ariel and Thelma and Geneva this?'

'I'm *using* them, to tell you. Right now, I'm using them. I'm focusing through them, with considerable effort on my part. And that's the only way. I can't tell them directly because they're a sub-part of me. A mind can't know its own thought processes directly. You I can tell, because you're infected too. There's a spanner in the works of your reality machine as well. But you stayed conscious, praise be for small mercies! Much more of this rupturing, and I won't be able to communicate at all lucidly. That's why I'm saying all this before your own tribe gets it together. Now, here's what I want you to do . . . And with your kind permission, I'll imprint it deep in you . . .'

The harlequin told her.

'Oh, my God!' exclaimed Robina.

'Exactly,' said Pansapiens. For he was God, of another time-stream . . .

Soon afterwards, Robina found herself stumbling about amidst grassy tussocks below a bushy hill. Cleopatra was clucking anxiously beside her, and comforting her by grooming her scalp. By now it was nearly noon, and Robina's hair was in a frightful tangle.

Chapter 27

Reverend Drew Hayes' alluring new secretary, with the bobbed peroxide hair, pert nose and noteworthy bosoms, sat in the inner sanctum of the mansion on Salvation Heights, most desirable suburb of Pompey.

She sat upon a warmly responsive leather armchair. This was actually Fred Fantazios in inanimate disguise. Fred could generally hold a pose without a quiver of reaction – playing the role of a boulder, for example, with all the timeless equanimity of stone. With Mentamorpha's thighs and buttocks pressed tightly into him, Fred was less submerged in perfect armchair passiveness. This armchair undulated gently.

Foobert growled a jealous protest now and then. He was the Doberman Pinscher currently reclining at Mentamorpha's feet, with his jaws upon his paws, and he seemed inclined to take a nip out of the lucky upholstery if Mentamorpha showed signs of squirming luxuriously upon it. Which, in fact, was far from her mind.

Behind the desk sat Prote, as Drew Hayes. He would far rather have worn the body of his secretary, but alas this could not be. As Drew Hayes, he was a burly, fat-jowled man. His chin was so deeply cleft that it looked as if a bolt had been hammered into it. His hair was chestnut, and his eyes lightning-blue. Large hairy hands were well designed for gripping lecterns and thumping on them.

He was engaged in neither activity at the present moment. He was polishing his coarse fingernails with an emery board, an activity quite at odds with his lectern-thumping demeanour. His secretary, on the other hand, had no desire to loll sybaritically in the armchair, letting it massage her legs and loins. *Her* climate of thought was that of the real Apostle Hayes.

Therefore she thumped the arm of the chair, bruising Fred's sensual illusions. The blow that fell was considerably less painful than if she had been wielding Hayes' own heavy fist.

'I'm *telling* you.' She spoke in the italicized sermon style which Harry Fullerton had borrowed from his spiritual father, the Reverend. 'The staff here suspect you have taken a *harlot*, a *Scarlet Woman*, all be it blonde, into your presence. You seclude yourself with her, as if you are engaged in secret *Fornication*, in Rutting Filth.'

Foobert woofed excitedly at this. The dog pawed the blue and cream Tientsin carpet, with a coiling dragon woven in it.

'Aw, come off it,' said Prote. 'We've got two chaperones all the time. Anyway, I'm not that way inclined.'

'But the staff do not know that this *Hell Hound* is a jealous chaperone. As for this chair, he is one Godforsaken *Sensualist!*' Mentamorpha kicked the chair with one of her stout brogues; these she wore, in preference to frivolous high-heeled shoes, as a sign of repentance, morality and scourging of the flesh. The chair winced, and became more rigid. 'At any moment this chair might turn into a lewd *sofa* for you to *seduce* me on – right here in the holy office.'

'Oh, I doubt Fred would want us two rolling about on top of him. That's more than flesh and blood could bear.'

'Marvin and Jones and Pastethorpe all think there's something *wrong* with you, holed up like this for weeks with a *woman*.'

'Hell, I'm – what's the word? – I'm in retreat. I'm meditating and praying. I'm gathering strength for the next stage of the Crusade.'

'Along with your Jezebel secretary? Along with your Whore of Babylon?'

'Somebody has to record my inspired thoughts.' Prote rummaged in a desk drawer and found a slim cigar, which he proceeded to wave about in an effeminate way, without troubling to light it.

'I'm wrestling with your soul, Mentamorpha. Or maybe I'm wrestling with my own. Shit, I *can't* be separated from you! I wouldn't know what to say.' Prote crushed the cigar into an onyx ashtray, though he had yet to light it.

The phone buzzed.

Mentamorpha swung the armchair around, forgetting for the moment that Fred Fantazios wasn't in a swivelling mode today. The chair squealed in protest before it could re-orient itself.

'Reverend Hayes' secretary speaking.'

'Visitor to see the Reverend,' came a surly drawl. Pastethorpe's.

'I'm sorry, but there are *no* appointments – '

'Just cut it out, Sister in the Lord. This visitor is Reverend Jake Hogan, all the way from Shiloh.'

'Oh my God.'

'Bless the Lord,' agreed Pastethorpe.

'Well, Reverend Hayes is *praying* for *guidance* right at this moment.'

'I bet.'

'Ask Reverend Hogan to wait five minutes, will you?' She cut the connexion. And whistled softly. 'Lo, the Third Apostle stands upon the doorstep. Ariel *will* be pleased.'

'Holy shit.' Prote adjusted his collar. 'Does this guy Hogan know me well?'

'As near as Matthew and Mark, or Luke and John. I *suspect* that the pious Pastethorpe asked Hogan to zip down here uninvited to check out your Scarlet Woman. So we'll take him quickly.' Mentamorpha stood up. 'Fred, shift yourself into a steel chair. Not uncomfortable-looking. Not so as Hogan's insulted or put off sitting in it. Let's see: something Scandinavian.'

Obediently the leather armchair began to convulse, thinning and tightening his upholstery towards a metallic texture.

'And you shift yourself too, Foobert. Move nearer the desk, and sort of shepherd Hogan this way. Do it subtly. Don't snarl. You'll have to help us gag him, so he doesn't get a chance to shout. When we've got him immobilized you, Prote, shift your shape to Hogan's. I'll dump Hayes, and map Hogan's mind instead.'

'Hey, but that leaves us with no Hayes afterwards.'

'So he used the emergency exit, on urgent business!' She nodded at the dummy wall panel – the secret of which she knew full well. 'That's why Hogan really came. See? Pastethorpe doesn't know the whole of it. Hogan will explain that as he's leaving.'

'Leaving? What, with Hayes' fucking secretary? And dog? And chair?'

'They'll go out the back way, idiot. Fred can grow some wheels, become a wheelchair. Foobert will push it.'

Unnoticed, the dog's muzzle had been contracting back into a human mouth, while displaced bones and tissue flowed upwards. Soon Foobert wore his regular human head, upon a dog's body. And he could speak, again.

'Oughtn't I to change back right now? I mean, I'll need *hands* if I'm going to help gag this Hogan. Not paws. It'll be a whole lot easier pushing a wheelchair, too, if I have upright posture.'

Mentamorpha was shocked to see the Doberman-man peering at her. This was ridiculously indiscreet.

She cried, 'Heel!' It was all she could think of, for the moment.

Obeying her command, Foobert began doggily trotting over.

'For Christ's sake, Foobert, I don't mean "heel" like that! I mean, not *now*! I mean, get your head straightened out!'

'Uh?'

'If Pastethorpe sees a total stranger in here – '

But at that moment the door opened unannounced and, uninvited, in came . . .

Foobert promptly turned tail, like the most cowardly guard dog ever seen. Diving under the desk, he hid his human head behind a waste bucket.

. . . in came a grizzly, granite-faced, white-haired man. His big flashing teeth were a veritable piano keyboard. He wore an impeccably tailored denim suit, with a shirt the pink and white of striped toothpaste.

Hogan's mouth sagged briefly (a silent crashing of chords) as he spied the Doberman, equally briefly. Then he caught sight of Mentamorpha. His mind rejected what he had glimpsed while Foobert scuttled for cover. Instead, his gaze photographed the seductive secretary, though not in X-ray style. In spite of her long modest skirt and stout brogues, she looked more like a casino pet than someone born again in the Lord. And yet . . . and yet, decided Hogan, there *was* a certain aura of moral rigour about the woman, as though she really had drunk at the fountain of the Apostle. Maybe Pastethorpe was mistaken in his suspicions. Yet surely friend Drew was acting naively, to say the least?

Ah, a good man might well appear naive to others who are less good!

Hogan closed the door behind him, admitting no one else. He strode to the desk.

'Blessings in the Lord, Brother Drew!'

Drew Hayes half-rose, then waved hastily at a large chair with shiny steel arms and legs, and a sagging leather seat.

'Blessings, blessings!' he bleated. His blue eyes wetly implored Jake to park himself.

Puzzled, Jake diverted himself towards the chair and thumped his bulk into it. The chair emitted an almost human groan.

Jake glanced significantly towards the secretary, dismissing her from the presence of the Apostles so they could get down to the real business, man to man. But as though she completely misunderstood the message, the woman moved behind his chair instead. Her hands were twitching about as though she wanted to massage the travel fatigue out of the neck and shoulders of Drew's most righteous buddy, as a family service. This rather confirmed Jake's earlier fears.

Drew stood up and circled round the desk. He poised himself beaming before Jake. His huge hands were playing with a lady's scarlet silk scarf. (The scarf of a Harlot! Jake revised his opinion steeply downhill.)

'Now, Fred! Take him!'

The steel chair arms writhed up and wrapped themselves around Jake's wrists. The chair legs manacled his ankles. As Jake opened his mouth to cry out, the masseuse behind him threw one arm around his throat, choking him. With her other hand she seized his hair, tugging his head back. Drew stuffed the scarlet scarf into Jake's open mouth, and began to fasten it tightly.

Yet Jake was not staring pop-eyed because of impending strangulation. He was staring because the Doberman had just at this moment emerged from under the desk – and the great black dog *had a human head*.

As the dog joined with the human couple and the animated chair in suppressing him, Jake uttered weird noises the like of which he had never heard issue from his mouth before.

The black dog with the human head was, of course, none other than the Devil.

Jake fought back valiantly. But the Devil Dog and the possessed couple and the chair, between them, forced his hands and then his feet together, to bind them with plastic cord. This done, Hayes shot the bolt on the door of his sanctum.

At any instant, Jake expected a flaming pit to open in the midst of the Tientsin carpet. But what actually happened next was far less explicable.

The Devil Dog drew back. He pranced upright, boxing the air with his paws. His human lips parted in a canine snarl.

'I'm *joined*!' he barked. 'The second tribe's joined! Stand by me, Fred!'

The chair was no longer gripping Jake, now that he was bound. It shuddered mightily beneath him. With one great convulsion it tossed his bound, gagged body off on to the carpet, severely winding him.

Lying gasping on his side, Jake noticed that the chair now possessed wheels. Which it hadn't, when he first sat in it. On these wheels it propelled itself towards Drew Hayes, bowling him over. Apparently forgetful of the fact that it had a human head, the Devil Dog bared its teeth and leapt upon Hayes, biting him in his right hand.

'Yow!' yelped Hayes.

Circling around smartly, the chair extruded one of its steel arms. This now terminated in a crudely fashioned metal hand. With this steel hand the chair began to throttle Hayes, while the dog held him down with its teeth.

'What's *with* you guys?' cried the secretary. 'Lord, this is a *Shame* upon the Sanctum! Foobert, *heel*! Fred Fantazios, just you *quit* it!'

She threw herself upon the dog. Releasing its grip on Hayes, the dog rolled over and slashed at the secretary with its powerful paws, tearing her long skirt from her body. Naked from the waist down, she battled on for a few seconds more, then hastily retreated round the desk. Yanking a heavy stainless steel cross from the wall, she brandished it.

Somewhat blue in the face, and with his right hand bleeding, Hayes managed to roll the murderous chair over and began battering it with his big left fist; though his blows did not seem quite as heavy or damaging as they ought.

Rather heavier, was the banging which commenced on the sanctum door.

'Oh my God.' The long-legged secretary hurled the cross away from her – smashing a window which, incidentally, led to the fire escape. Swinging round, she fiddled with the wall. A whole panel slid aside, and through this opening she disappeared. Drew Hayes, blood dripping from his hand, and the self-propelled wheelchair, and the man-headed dog all followed her pell-mell, still scrapping with each other. (But from his position on the floor, cheek pressed to the carpet, Jake Hogan couldn't see the secret exit open and shut. All he saw was a confusion of feet and paws and wheels disappearing round the desk.) The panel slid shut only moments before the bolt burst from the sanctum door, admitting Pastethorpe, Jones and Marvin.

These three Godly Guardians gazed round the sanctum in bewilderment. Reverend Jake Hogan lay squirming, trussed up on the floor, infernal hysteria in his eyes. A torn skirt lay near him. Nowhere were Reverend Hayes or his secretary to be seen. (Nor, for that matter, were his flashy leather armchair or his savage Doberman, though these absences would take a little longer to register.)

Pastethorpe undid the scarlet gag.

'Look at 'em!' begged Hogan.

'Look at who?'

Jones ran to the broken window and looked out.

'The dog with the head of the Devil! And the living wheelchair! And the harlot naked from the waist down!'

'Reverend Hayes and his woman didn't go out the window,' called Jones. 'Not unless they flew. Or fell a long way. Fire escape's still up.'

'Yes, they flew! They flew out!' screamed Hogan. 'Those naked whoring legs, and those wheels, and the head of a man on a dog! The Devil and all his Works!'

Reverend Jake Hogan began to froth at the mouth, and rave incoherently. Pastethorpe thought it wiser not to undo his hands just yet.

Chapter 28

Prote, in the form of Reverend Hayes, and the skirtless Mentamorpha raced into the parking lot by the Salvation Heights Gourmet Food-Mart, where they had left the God Nut camper. There weren't *too* many people about. And just possibly this half-naked blonde sprinter might be a candidate cheerleader for the Spiritual Crusade, being put through her paces by Reverend Hayes on a training run. On the principle of the Emperor's New Clothes, witnesses tended to see the woman as wearing very skimpy running shorts rather than nylon briefs.

In hot pursuit lumbered a Doberman Pinscher, who had by now mostly regained his canine features. He wasn't running in as sprightly or bounding a manner as such a dog ought to. Yet that was all right too; obviously the dog needed a workout, though really it ought to have been on a lead.

Lastly down the hill, apparently out of control, careered an unoccupied invalid chair . . .

Prote and Mentamorpha scrambled into the cab of the camper – Mentamorpha taking the wheel side – and slammed and locked the doors.

Mentamorpha shut her eyes in concentration.

'I've got a strong feeling we ought to get back to the Farm right away! Oh, there's *Strife*, and there will be *Bloody Blows*! Shit, I'd better dump Drew Hayes out of my head. He's confusing me. Will you please stop looking so much like him, Prote?'

The Doberman began yapping and leaping around the vehicle.

'What's gone wrong?'

She concentrated.

'I dunno. It's the battle of the Lapiths and the Centaurs all over again, whatever that was.'

The dog's muzzle snarled at the window. Teeth grated on the impact-proof glass.

'Should we take them with us?'

'They've become our enemies, Prote. It's their tribe against our

152

tribe.' Mentamorpha opened her eyes again, and squealed to see the rabid hound.

Just then, the wheelchair cornered sharply and crashed into a row of supermarket trolleys waiting to be pushed back into the Gourmet Food-Mart. The collision stunned Fred Fantazios. To regain his bearings, hastily he adopted the protective camouflage of the nearest inanimate object, which happened to be the silver shopping chariot directly in front of him.

Mentamorpha started the engine, and backed out with a shriek of rubber. Foobert chased the camper some way down the street, but he was soon outdistanced. His muscles were all one big ache now, and his heart was pounding fit to burst. His tail between his legs, he slunk back to the Food-Mart, just in time to see an attendant in a sky-blue uniform straining as he shoved the whole line of trolleys in through the doors of the Food-Mart.

Foobert took up watch outside the automatic glass doors, pretending to be hitched there waiting for his mistress.

Shoppers came and went, eyeing the sprawling, tongue-lolling dog indignantly.

Presently a stout woman with blue-rinsed hair, wearing bell-bottom jeans and a short mink jacket, marched indoors. She jerked Fred Fantazios free of the waiting trolleys, hung her zebra-skin purse over him, and wheeled him along the shelves. She piled him high with cans of tacos and enchiladas and tortillas, with bottles of gherkins and pepper sauce and Montezuma dressing . . .

Inexplicably – though quite explicable by the fact that Fred wasn't wholly a deep shopping trolley, except as regards appearance and touch – cans started to roll off him, as if defying gravity. Swearing, the woman threw them back hard again, into Fred's bowed back. Crippled, Fred rolled on, his burden increasing.

Soon after, a truck from the dog pound drew up in front of the Food-Mart. Foobert took to his heels, pursued by a dog catcher brandishing a pole with a noose on the end.

Initially, Brutus had been doubtful as to the merits of returning to the Farm. The superchimps had proved, during the night raid on Stenton, that they could replenish the larder of the camper; and that Boadicaea could drive it well enough. Yet there were only three gallons of fuel remaining in the tank, and unattended pumps were always locked up. A hold-up conducted by a pistol-toting apeman was bound to attract attention; and they had no desire to go public yet.

Besides, they had achieved their primary goal. For Robina had gone right through her change without being submerged the whole time in unconsciousness.

Robina had indeed changed, and become new-Robina. Yet she hadn't altered physically to any remarkable extent – beyond becoming somewhat leaner, with less mountainous bosoms; and this loss of weight may have been due simply to the stringencies of life in the wild without benefit of glucose and proper bed rest.

Like Thelma Harvey before her, Robina had come to sense through her fingers and her toes an intimate linkage with her tribe thirty miles away (and two of them even further away in Pompey).

Though she had been wide awake during her encounter with the Godly harlequin who called himself Pansapiens, the experience had soon taken on in retrospect the dimensions of a delirium – a derangement of the senses that was perhaps an essential part of the change-fugue. Had not Joan of Arc heard voices? Had not Moses met a burning bush which spoke to him? While Joseph Smith had been accosted by an angel with the uninviting name of Moroni. Had these three actually experienced unwitting, incoherent leakages from the collective human race of the alternative time-stream? This seemed far-fetched.

Yet Cleopatra smelled, if not a rat, at least something 'which does not belong'; and when Robina had done her best, subsequently, to explain to her metapongid guardian what she had seen and heard of Pansapiens, the response had flashed back:

'True! Very true! Apples on banana plants! Growing in *another* garden. Cross-fertilizing. This must stop! Or there will be no true apples, no true bananas. Only crazy bananapples.

'Alas,' Cleo had then signed, '*we* have no tree of family. No hope of filling the world is ours. But we will make our way on our own, till we die out. *You* must lock the bananapple family away, where it can do no harm.'

So Cleo must have argued against Brutus, in favour of returning at least temporarily to the Farm.

Robina wondered how much the superchimps actually understood of all this. Yet they seemed both brave and resolute. She herself now felt imprinted with a sense of mission which she sincerely felt owed as much to the superchimps' intuitions as to her own brush with Pansapiens – who might or might not really exist, as the true God, on the flipside of reality.

Twitching her fingers and toes experimentally – and because of this occasionally braking unexpectedly or putting on sudden spurts of speed – Robina had driven the camper back to the Farm. There her tribe awaited her: butterfly-winged Icara, flaring Phaethon, the truly reborn Harry Fullerton, Hacker the garage owner and thirty-odd more, all waiting to be pitted against the first tribe. For that was the course events must take. Without a question.

Robina had barrelled the camper straight through the main gate while her superchimp passengers made 'see no evil' gestures in case any of the shatter-proof glass shattered. The gate had yielded easily enough. It had already been wrecked once, on their way out days before.

They had driven at speed – as a siren began to *whoop* – down past the grazing Guernsey cows and the horse paddock, till they arrived at the ranch house. Here they skidded to a halt outside the selfsame French windows they had left by. While Robina had sat revving the engine, Caesar and Brutus had burst the windows open. Brutus returned bearing the *Sansevieria* plant: that immortal cluster of vegetable swords which Robina knew was able, for some reason, to halt the mighty Geneva in her tracks. This, and this alone. Back in the camper, Brutus had sniffed the sharpest spike of all, and kissed his fingers appreciatively; a trace of Geneva's blood still remained.

Robina had gunned the camper along past the whooping watch-tower, and as they passed by a single dart pinged off the front bumper. No doubt this was aimed at the tyre; not even the stupidest of guards could hope to anaesthetize a charging vehicle.

At the entry of the maze she had braked. With the *Sansevieria* clutched in one hand, and a flashlight from the camper's tool kit in the other, she had dashed inside. Then Brutus and Cleo had taken the lead.

Already Robina had known in her toes and fingers that her tribe

155

were running, too. They were all converging on the hollow stone lion at the base of the monumental column known as 'the Lighthouse'. For that was where the tunnel which linked the ranch house with the bomb-proof cavern under the upland sent up a flight of steps to the surface.

Aided by the flashlight, they made their way rapidly for a mile along the brick-walled tunnel. This was the dimension of a dry sewer, or a subway tunnel minus the rails. Certainly it was wide enough to accept a convoy of small Japanese supply trucks driving at speed; and the further they penetrated, the more Robina feared this eventuality. Ariel had forbidden hot pursuit into the estate; but did that apply below ground too?

When they reached the base of the stairway, ahead of them the tunnel still burrowed on dimly towards the cavern. Robina paused. She noticed steel doors, which could only be blast doors, recessed into the wall both before and beyond the stairway.

Wheels poked from the wall for the manual operation of these doors. In addition, two dusty glass plates shielded red switches, like fire alarms. In an emergency it must be possible to slam the doors shut instantly. But how? By explosive charges? No, that would concuss whoever pulled the switch. The means was hidden in the wall.

Robina considered the door which would block access from the direction of the ranch house. In the torchlight she found some rubble and an abandoned crowbar. With a half-brick she smashed the glass. Throwing the switch, she jumped clear.

A hesitation . . . a preliminary hiss . . . then a *woosh* of air, as though she was standing beside a vintage steam engine . . . was followed by a thunderclap of steel as the blast door sprang shut. Robina was stunned for a time as much by the booming reverberations as by the original bang.

As soon as the echoes died down, she handed the flashlight to Cleo. Pulling out the crowbar from the rubble, she jammed it into the winding wheel and began to lever. Brutus and Boadicaea joined her. They heaved. Suddenly the whole wheel sheared clean off its base and clattered to the floor, narrowly missing their toes as they all danced back.

Now that she was satisfied that anyone fleeing down the stairway would only have one direction to head in – namely, towards the cavern – Robina led her escort up the steps.

A tiny stone cave capped the flight; and this was the hollow inside of the lion. It was Caesar who had discovered its secret one day when he had swung playfully on the jutting stone tail. Robina could now see little discs of daylight through the lion's nostrils and through the hole at the back of its slightly open mouth.

Most of her tribe were gathered outside. She felt them. She heard them murmuring.

Crowding into the lion's belly in a dense clump of flesh and fur, the superchimps and Robina tried to pivot it, heaving and thrusting against its inner flanks. The lion seemed disinclined to move, since they were all pushing at cross purposes.

Since she couldn't sign to them in the gloom, Robina pushed her helpers back down the steps with her hands. She hollered through the hole in the lion's throat:

'Pull my tail!' And the stone lion spoke unto her tribe. Hastily, she ducked down again.

Soon the lion swung round, disclosing the blue sky. It was Mr Hacker who hauled on the stone tail. By now he was a powerful centaur. But he had dug his hooves unnecessarily hard into the turf, and slithered sideways as the statue shifted. Really, it was quite easy to move the lion, once you had the knack.

Man and boy, Mr Hacker had been obsessed with horse-power, though always of the mechanical variety – a very different breed from that doted on by Mrs Sandra Glass of the Blue House. Yet now he was one horse-power from the navel downwards for the rest of his life. To his surprise he felt profoundly satisfied by this change. And he thought he understood why. In recent years he had begun to worry deeply about the world's oil supplies. This had led him into religious excesses, such as listening to the God Nut radio station in Pompey, hoping for news that the Arabs had been wiped out in some heaven-sent plague, thus liberating the oil fields.

He had dropped all that now like a load of horse shit.

True, at first he had been shocked to find himself equipped with four legs. Yet as soon as he had test-galloped himself, he had found the whole experience far more satisfying than merely sitting at a wheel. *This* must have been his inner, secret dream all along. All his mechanical tinkering had been mere sublimation. In the old days he had often had nightmares about trying to outrace a herd of stallions, with his dream body perched on top of increasingly preposterous and troublesome machines. Now his fantasies were more of Sandra Glass in her future metamorphosis as the perfect female centaur.

Yet at the same time Hacker still felt a lingering sense of guilt about his change – as though such nude equine muscularity as his was *too much*; as though he might somehow be punished for kicking over the traces . . .

Robina and the superchimps clambered into the sunshine. Robina twitched a finger at Mr Hacker approvingly; and he whinnied back. To his surprise; for normally he spoke.

Chapter 29

The lighthouse rose a hundred feet, commanding all but the heights of the estate – so long as you had the eyesight of a telescope. Its Doric column bellied out midway then tapered again, to provide an illusion of straight lines. But the illusion failed; the column seemed gently pregnant.

Its connexion with the sea came from the beaked stone prows of ships which protruded from the shaft – and from the windows which encircled the top. Below those windows ran the carved and gilded legend: *Non nisi grandia canto*. 'None but heroic deeds I sing.' The mute songstress of these deeds was a statue of Heroic Poetry who stood upon the cupola. A lightning conductor poked from her head like an aerial. With her right hand she pointed down at the legend. She wore on her face the puzzled frown of a stranded elevator lady from Ancient Rome.

Taking the statue's words to heart, Robina rallied the tribe.

Climbing on to Mr Hacker's horse-back, she then led them all down from the Lighthouse towards the Temple of Venus two miles away. All, that is, apart from Phaethon. Though he was one of her most powerful weapons, a devious prompting of instinct made her leave him behind. She commanded him to climb the Lighthouse and

158

flame on, come evening, at her signal. Up at those topmost windows, Phaethon would then transform the column into a genuine Pharos – one designed to lure lost navigators with its beacon and its bait, wrecking them below.

As Robina rode at a gentle walk down towards the temple, she extended her little toes to touch Foobert and Fred Fantazios far away.

Though it was still bright daylight, an owl awoke and screeched three times.

It had begun.

Why exactly it had begun, her tribe were no more sure than the Lapiths and the Centaurs were quite sure why their murderous battle had started at the wedding feast of Hippodame – except that a madness hounded them, and their new sense of tribal identity persuaded them.

Maybe the statue of Heroic Poetry atop the Doric column would have sung out, had her stone lips been able to shape words, to the effect that a God, a natural force of a higher kind, had driven them all mad – so that they swore allegiance to crime: the crime of betrayal of Ariel, the Founder, with the result that his science, and Ohira's, would be overthrown and defeated.

No doubt, in Second Time, the Great God Pansap now relaxed. While the silver egg took off for the stars, eventually to split him healthily in half . . .

'We'll replace the main gate with *sheet steel*,' promised Maccoby, on screen. 'They won't bust out again. Do you want an armed team in the grounds, sir?'

'Why the hell should I? Haven't they come back of their own free will? Isn't that a good sign? Reuben, I very much misdoubt your desire to introduce a goon squad on *this* side of the fence.'

'Woe,' called Silvester dolefully from outside the door. 'Chaos will reign, till all of us are thrust beneath the Earth. With the roof of the world above me, how shall I ever grow to my full height?'

Geneva laughed dismissively.

'I can pick Robina Weber up under one arm.'

Argus stepped round the tree-man.

'I can't see her or the pongos anywhere. I'm blind to them.'

'That's because they're underground, dummy. They're still in the tunnel. You'll see them soon enough, when they pop out. So keep an eye on the Lighthouse. As soon as you can, tell me what's been happening with Robina.'

'But I've *told* you: I can't far-see and past-see at the same time. Should I go up there in person? That Lighthouse seems like a popular venue at the moment.'

'Eh?'

'The others – the ones who aren't in our network – all seem to have headed up there.'

'Then Robina must be the new Joiner! Why, that's wonderful. That explains why she came back: she couldn't keep away. Why didn't you tell me before?'

'I thought they were just organizing a party or festival or something. Should I go up there?'

'No, not right away. Let's give her a chance to get it all together. What do you think, Thelma?'

Thelma had been standing abstractedly, twitching her fingers and toes as if she was operating some invisible abacus.

'Doom,' pronounced Silvester.

Thelma linked him to all the others of her tribe. No words existed for what was going to happen – so that it could not be foretold – yet for a time everyone felt the tension of a storm about to break. The imminence of lightning about to blast a tree.

This lightning would not kill the tree. Yet it would certainly stunt its growth. The tree would be buried underneath an avalanche . . .

But the sense of foreboding remained undefined. As for lightning, Ariel was the only local source of lightning that they knew. The second tribe remained opaque.

Thelma disengaged from Silvester.

'I think we're *jealous*. The change is about to give birth to a second child – one who'll share the place with us on an equal footing. Deep in our hearts, we're uneasy about it. We mustn't be.'

'Well, sir?' asked Maccoby.

Suddenly Silvester pointed an accusing branch through the door at the screen.

'And *he* will be our jailer! Only the chimps will go free!'

160

Thelma linked herself briefly to Silvester again. She could make nothing of this prophecy, though, since neither could Silvester.

'How soon will Drew Hayes be through his change?' Ariel was asking.

'Shiba says a couple more days. That's par for the course. With some good make-up, and clever tailoring to hide that camel hump on his back and his two extra arms, he should be able to pass for the old Drew Hayes.'

'Dromedary hump,' Geneva corrected him. 'Camels have two humps, dromedaries have one.'

'Well, whatever. You can really get the God Nuts to change their tune, then! Bring us recruits by the busload.'

'So long as Robina agrees,' said Thelma. 'Hayes is one of hers, remember?'

'No, he ain't,' said Ariel. 'He'll be part of the *third* tribe. Anyway, even if he was one of hers, why shouldn't he agree?' Ariel bristled electrically. 'Hell's teeth, that's the whole *plan*. By the busload . . . I like it, Reuben! We'll get the changed Hayes to invite all the Big Names who subscribe to the God Nut movement in this area. He'll invite them for, uh, a country retreat . . . A fortnight or so of prayer and rededication of themselves. That's it. No alcoholic beverages served, of course. Just plain Diet Pepsi.'

'Oh, lord!'

'Thelma?'

'Prote and Mentamorpha are in trouble.'

'Have the God Nuts rumbled them?'

'Yes . . . No, that isn't it! Well, it's that *too*. But – ' She abstracted herself. 'I can feel them fighting. Prote's hurt his hand. *How?* It's that dog! It's Foobert! Foobert attacked them. God, it's a shambles. They'd just got one of the other Apostles successfully tied down – and suddenly it all went wrong. Foobert's turned rabid!'

'He's turned into a rabbit?'

'*Rabid*, I said! The chair's gone mad too. It's swung against them.'

Icara the butterfly-woman, returning from scouting out the land, fluttered in to land on Mr Hacker's rump just behind Robina.

Having failed to notice her eccentric landing approach, the centaur switched his tail, nearly knocking Icara off him, before he realized that she wasn't an oversize horse-fly. Robina slapped Mr Hacker's flank, at once soothing and admonishing him. She remembered that she could do this just as easily by crooking her finger.

Robina had already scried the general disposition of Tribe One from the air, while Icara flew erratically about. The first tribe was quite widely scattered. Only the command nucleus of Thelma, Ariel, Geneva, Silvester and Argus was gathered at the Temple of Venus. Robina listened intently to Icara's somewhat flighty verbal report, to confirm her own impressions from the air, then swung her main picket line eastwards intending to come up on the temple from its southern side – so that they could herd that nucleus, like hounds herding deer, towards the pitfall below the Lighthouse.

'Good work, Icara. Fly back. Watch whether any more of them gather as we get nearer.'

'It isn't so easy for me! Not to fly a bee-line. I get distracted. By anything! I'm a creature of caprice.'

'So are we all, dear. Far more than you realize. Just do your best.'

Robina fingered and toed her troops out through the glades.

The fat former God Nut woman had changed into a great white grub or caterpillar, perhaps prior to becoming a winter chrysalis out of which something more elegant would emerge in the spring. She humped her bulk along at surprising speed on twenty or thirty short legs, crashing through the bushes.

She was the first to start some quarry. Shetani darted out of the boscage, squealing in panic when she saw what was bearing down on her. The Unit darted this way and that irrationally.

The grub-woman reared, waving ten or twelve legs in the air. When the chameleon-pig ill-advisedly scampered under her, the great grub squelched down upon the hindquarters of the Unit. Shrieking, Shetani the rider popped right out of her crushed mount. The rider fell in the grass. She jerked and twitched and began crying out in her native Makonde tongue.

The grub-woman swung towards her. And here, for the rider, was a *real* shetani, ambushing her in the Bush! As large as a cow, with so many legs! Scrambling up, Shetani scuttled out of the way in terror.

Down at the temple, Shetani's terror infected Thelma. Thelma was already fleeing for her life, in two other aspects, pursued by a savage Doberman and a runaway wheelchair . . .

As dusk drew its mantle down over the day, the spearhead of the second tribe at last arrived to the south of the temple. They halted in horseshoe formation. Robina had taken her time with the advance. The longer that her picket line spent on flushing out isolated members of Thelma's tribe, the more fear and confusion they spread.

Well alerted to the threat by now, Ariel waited outside the temple on Geneva's shoulder, charged with lightning, ready to launch himself. Yet still he refused Maccoby's offer of a peace-keeping force.

Impatiently Geneva stamped the turf. She balled and unballed her fists. Nixy the water nymph, flushed from a pool earlier on, was clutching hold of the lesser satyr at last, to his confused satisfaction. Argus gazed in horror with all his eyes, straining against the decline of day for each scattered photon of warning. He was waiting for the first direct sighting of Robina; then he could past-see what had come over her. Silvester stood to one side, his branches raised, ready to bring them down stunningly on enemy heads. Thelma was trying to control herself. She was infected by gusts of hysteria from Shetani, who was now reduced to helpless child size, and loose in the darkening, night-mare haunted woods. How Thelma wished that she could strike off the finger and the toe which linked her to this hellish delirium! Yet, even though Shetani played havoc with her concentration, still Thelma strove to rally her own tribe to her. At least a dozen of her network had already tangled with Robina's forces. Most had fled; some had failed to flee. As a result of these encounters, two of her toes were dead. This upset Thelma's sense of balance, and temporarily robbed her of contact with two more members of her tribe who were paired on a finger-toe basis . . .

Eventually Robina rode into the temple glade on Mr Hacker's back. Six of her tribe flanked her. Harry Fullerton, former God Nut but now a Christian devil with horns and a barbed tail, advanced ahead. As did another ex-God Nut spy, now an Angel of Righteousness. Both angel and devil clutched wooden knobkerries broken from the forest.

Ariel promptly launched himself from Geneva towards a plane tree. Grasping the lowest branch, he scurried inwards then shinned up higher and higher and crept out along a limb.

'Why, Robina? Why?' he cried, in as loud a voice as he could muster.

Either rebellious Robina failed to hear his little voice, or else she ignored it.

Ariel let go of his perch. In a long glide he swept down across the glade. Geneva also charged at the same moment, bellowing a war cry. Robina, for her part, spurred Mr Hacker forward with her heels.

Ariel's glide carried him over Harry Fullerton. The devil thrashed the air with his cudgel. Ariel, pulling out of his dive, climbed clear – and merely touched the cudgel with his fingertip. Lightning clove the wood. The devil collapsed, stunned.

Ariel reached the safety of another bough, scrambled higher, and hunched there quickly accumulating more energy.

With one careless fist Geneva swatted away the club of the Angel of Righteousness; and the force of her charge knocked him sideways. Without breaking step she rushed on, on collision course with the centaur, who was now at half gallop.

From behind Mr Hacker's human torso Robina suddenly produced the *Sansevieria* in its pot. Leaning forward, while clutching Mr Hacker around the waist with her other arm, she rode at tilt towards Geneva. The blades of the plant jutted ahead like an already splintered lance.

Too late, Geneva saw the weapon she most feared.

A moment later, it impaled her in the breast.

Even so, sheer momentum still carried her on into the centaur, tumbling him, unseating Robina.

Robina held on long enough to slither around Mr Hacker's torso and avoid being crushed by his fall. Since she had received some Judo instruction from Dr Shiba, in case her superchimps ever misbehaved grossly, she performed a roll – and came up awkwardly, but still came up, pulling the pistol from her waistband.

The sword-plant had driven deeper this time than on the previous occasion. Blood visibly soaked Geneva's twice-rent robe. Even so, the plant could *still* hardly have dealt a fatal injury. Yet Geneva reacted as before. She behaved as if the leaves had been tipped with instant poison, and all her strength had flowed out of her wound. She wandered helplessly, holding herself, murmuring, 'Josie . . . Alison . . .'

Mr Hacker scrambled up. But he had sprained a fetlock. So now he proceeded, in a three-legged way, to herd the stricken Geneva back towards the temple, using her body as a shield. Ariel swooped overhead again – and Robina tracked him with her pistol – but he could not use his sting because of Geneva.

From the instant that the *Sansevieria* had impacted in the giantess, Thelma the Joiner had felt dark Death marching through her mind – draining her, dimming her lights. Paralysis and despair invaded her, in addition to the panic which Shetani was broadcasting.

'Ah, *now* I see!' exclaimed Argus, close beside her. 'Robina met a . . . *what on earth was it?* No, it *wasn't* of Earth. Not of this Earth. And it charged her with the task of . . . But it came out of *us*! We were its route to the surface. Oh, it's so dim. It's all in the corners of my eyes. Oh, give me the *light* to see!'

The other side of Robina's horseshoe emerged from the woods, blocking the entrance to the temporarily deserted temple. A two-headed ogre who had, unbeknownst to his recruiters, been schizophrenic before his change now barred the way indoors. As did a silver-skinned, sexless person with large, deepset eyes and the merest hint of nose or ears. This was Gorgo, a former devotee of flying saucer cults, who had turned into a humanoid ufonaut. Gorgo could paralyse or hypnotize people with his gaze, and even disrupt electrical circuits from a distance.

These two personages stepped forth just as Ariel was gliding down from the plane tree again, this time intending to sweep in through the temple doorway to call for assistance from Maccoby.

Ariel extended his fingers to shock them. Gorgo locked his gaze with Ariel's, and blocked his lightning. The ogre caught Ariel in his arms.

Into the temple ran Gorgo, to stare at the TV console where the image of Maccoby was fretting impatiently. At a gesture from Robina, the ogre bore the paralysed Ariel inside the temple too, to be hypnotized.

'Oh yes, give us light!' cried Thelma, as the darkness deepened around her and within her.

And a light blossomed in the distance. It was as though a bright new planet had appeared, or a nearby star had flared up.

Thelma fled from the vicinity of the temple. She began running through the woods towards that beacon. And as she ran, so her sprinting toes and her outstretched fingers drew the rest of her tribe who were still at liberty inexorably towards that focal point from wherever they were . . .

The rout had begun.

Chapter 30

Shortly after her breathless arrival at the Lighthouse, many more of Thelma's tribe joined her and milled about there. Members of the second tribe, hot on the tail of the first tribe, penned and corralled Thelma's people.

Thelma gazed up at Phaethon behind glass high at the top of the column. He was starting to flicker and die down. Before long the human torch was all but extinguished. But it was too late, now, to escape from the trap he had set.

Mr Hacker limped up, pushing drooping Geneva ahead of him. A woman with an elephant's trunk of a nose had sniffed out Shetani *en route*. She came cradling the miserable rider, bereft forever of her mount. She thrust the black stick-person into the lesser satyr's arms.

And finally the ogre raced from the woods, bearing a dopy Ariel. Robina accompanied him, with flashlight and pistol. The stone lion still stood aside, uncovering the top of the steps. Here the ogre deposited Ariel, pointing him down towards that underworld where he had once planned to take refuge from any outside war. But now he was a refugee, instead, in a war which had rolled across his own lands.

Ariel soon recovered from his Gorgo-induced paralysis, but a different sort of lethargy overcame him – the lethargy of defeat. Robina tossed the flashlight to Argus. He caught it gratefully, for he craved light right now as much as Thelma craved it. With her pistol, Robina brusquely gestured him to lead the descent down the steps. As Argus began to vanish underground, Thelma heedlessly followed the light he held, with Ariel clutching her hem.

And so, with some of the changed people crying adieu to the grounds which they could visit no more, one by one the first tribe plunged beneath the earth. Silvester was the last to depart, stumbling awkwardly on his roots.

Mr Hacker backed up against the stone tail and swung the lion back into position. The stairs were capped.

In the deepening darkness the burlier members of Thelma's tribe went in search of stones and logs to pile around the lion. Phaethon descended from the pharos; he did his best to illuminate their labours at half-power.

By now it was night.

In spite of their joy at being joined together in Robina, many of her tribe were frankly puzzled.

'Why?' she heard.

'Why?'

'Why?'

She asked herself the same question. And it did indeed seem as if a holy madness had come over them all during the past few hours.

Robina vaguely recalled why that was. But it did not matter why. How could she *sustain* it? That was the question, now.

She linked herself to Mr Hacker and Harry Fullerton, and to the Angel of Righteousness and the grub-woman. The wonder of the change had rewired their minds. Yet there was still a depth of passionate bigotry locked in their memories. Locked. It was sealed off almost as firmly as Ariel and his tribe were now sealed off from the surface.

'Remember yourselves,' whispered Robina. 'Remember.'

She drew upon Gorgo's power of hypnosis – the power possessed by fantastic silver aliens, of whom he was now one.

'Remember!'

And the seal was torn. Mr Hacker reared, whinnying. The grub-woman thumped herself upon the ground in execration. Harry Fullerton thrashed his devil's tail. The Angel of Righteousness cried havoc.

'Peace!' commanded Robina. And far away in the Pompey dog pound even Foobert felt peaceful. (He was reluctant to shift back into a man since he had been penned up with a bitchy alsatian. Anyway, he might be taken for a werewolf. A flood of horror movies had alerted the public to just such a possibility. If the dog pound guard saw Foobert shifting shape, he would probably shoot him . . .)

As Robina shared the feelings of the ex-God Nuts around, a moan rose from the tribe, even from carefree Icara.

'We have *sinned*,' Robina explained carefully. 'We have strayed from our way like lost sheep. We have undone those things that we ought not to have undone: the corsets of our bodies. Yet we can *redeem* ourselves. We have already begun to, by casting those other possessed mortals down into *Hell*. We must keep them there forever, to stop Hell itself from bursting forth. By doing this – and by hiding ourselves away from the sight of healthy men and women for the rest of our mortal lives – we shall become the blessed of God. We shall be his Saints and Martyrs. Though only He will know it.

'And he will reward us for our sacrifice.

'For God is immutable. He made us in His image. He doesn't like change. Change comes from the Devil! Change bends the image of God. And we are wretchedly bent. But in our wretchedness is our hope.

'Oh yes, the Devil is the cause of change! His is the theory of evolution that pollutes our schools. For if God made us perfect, wherefore should we change?

'We can't worship God in ourselves. Not now! But we can still worship Him in all the rest of the human race. They will stay the same for ever and for ever, unchangingly!

'We nearly tumbled into a Pit, my friends. How narrowly, by His Grace, did we hold back so that now instead we stand around the lip of the Pit, guarding it!'

She led them all in an impromptu hymn of thanksgiving. It rose easily to her lips:

> *'The form of Man is perfect,*
> *'It comes from God above!*
> *'And if you don't believe it,*
> *'Then you deny His love!*

> *'Our arms and legs and noses*
>> *'Our brains and breasts and bums*
> *'Are measured out in Heaven*
>> *'Where God does his sums.*
>
> *'Satan is a shifty one;*
>> *'He wants us all to change.*
> *'In labs and schools and test-tubes*
>> *'He works us to derange.*
>
> *'The race of Man forever*
>> *'Shall keep its perfect form,*
> *'So let us praise this watchword:*
>> *'Adherence to the norm.*
>
> *'Yet we are changed, and fallen,*
>> *'In an Eden without Eve.*
> *'Unlike the sinful Adam*
>> *'Here we must never leave.*
>
> *'But when we go to Heaven*
>> *'He will give us back our shapes,*
> *'For they're all still stored up there,*
>> *'On God's own golden tapes . . .'*

To begin with, the singing was a little ragged. But it soon gathered strength and co-ordination.

Robina dismissed the majority of her tribe till mid-morning prayers the following day, and set off again for the Temple of Venus, which she had decided she would probably rename the Chapel of Conformity. Gorgo accompanied her, and Phaethon lit the way as well as he could.

As for those obscene murals, she would most likely leave them intact. Conceivably there would need to be periodic orgies of self-disgust and mutual abuse (though without conception), orgies during which they would blaspheme each other with their altered bodies. Thus by opposites they could worship the true Godly form that they would all regain in another world, when the whole misconceived experiment had died away. Robina knew there was another world somewhere. So it must be beyond the grave, mustn't it?

As they walked down through the black woods, inside Phaethon's faint halo of light, she gave Gorgo new instructions.

Arriving at the temple, they found Maccoby still staring impassively out of the screen. Gorgo had implanted the suggestion, earlier, that the security chief was watching a ball game.

Chapter 31

During breakfast, the screen bleeped. Still chewing a bacon and waffle sandwich, Robina took the call. Pulling a stool up behind her, Gorgo her mesmerizing chamberlain peered over her shoulder.

Maccoby looked dog-tired, but smugly gratified. If any suspicions lurked in him that his actions had not arisen, quite naturally, out of longstanding conspiracy with Robina, he did not betray them.

'Morning, ma'am. The limo team just called from Pompey. They're in position outside the dog pound. Soon as it opens for business, they'll claim the Doberman. They're heading over to the Food-Mart next, to collect that trolley. They'll just load it up with a few things and wheel it through the checkout. But they want to know: how do they tell which trolley's which?'

'No problem, Reuben. Fred changed back for a while last night. He needed a meal. He ate a lot of herrings in wine sauce from those ring-pull cans, and he drank a few cartons of pineapple juice. The litter is all in his trolley. You can bet nobody else'll take it, looking like that.'

'Wait though. The store detective might wonder about a pile of empty cans. Mice don't have fingers.'

'Ah . . . Look, Reuben: send the Mercedes over to the Food-Mart *first*, in time for it opening. Then call by the dog pound, second. An hour or so won't matter. They have to keep strays for at least a week before they destroy them. I think.'

Robina finished eating her sandwich while Maccoby was relaying the change of plan.

'Prote and Mentamorpha ought to be near the Farm by now,' he reminded her. 'If they're coming.'

Which meant that the stone lion would have to be unblocked for them. But then blocked up again, for good. Perhaps cemented in position.

'I've got an interception team out on the road, and the chopper's up. They've got the licence number of that camper. But there's no sign of them.'

Was it possible that Prote and Mentamorpha could take off on their own, as a husband and wife team? If that happened, Thelma would still have a couple of fingers stuck in the pie of the outside world. Two fingers weren't sufficient to exert very much leverage. Not enough to topple the stone lion.

Yet it would mean that a shape-shifter was loose in the world . . .

Robina crossed herself, devoutly.

'Listen to me, Reuben: if they aren't back by tomorrow you will hire a detective agency to look for Mentamorpha. Don't bother describing Prote – he could look like anyone. Anyway, I'm sure those two'll stick together. They're complementary. But keep the agency *at it* till they find Mentamorpha, even if it takes the next five years.'

'Will do. Now, other matters, Robina. I've locked Shiba and Ohira up in the old chimp compound, as instructed.'

'That's where those hands of Satan will stay.'

'I personally wrecked the lab. I burnt all the records. I poured all the Diet Pepsi into a bath of nitric acid.'

'Excellent. Have you checked the access codes I gave you for the rest of King Enterprises?'

By way of answer, Maccoby grinned broadly.

'In effect, you're the head of the whole operation now, Reuben. You control the voting stock. But please remember this: you are not a very clever head.' Robina snapped her fingers, and rapped out sharply, 'Egnach! Egnach!' (which was change, backwards).

This was Maccoby's cue phrase. He lolled obediently with zombie stare.

'If ever you fail me, Ariel comes up like an imp out of Hell. He will be most angry with you, Reuben. You will *always* fear this. But I shall keep Ariel safely locked away from you. Thus you can enjoy your reign. You will call us every Sunday morning regularly at ten A.M. for special therapy. And give thanks to the Lord that your shape is still the same, and your soul untwisted. Now, Reuben, gaze into Gorgo's eyes . . .'

Gorgo humped his stool around next to Robina.

PART FIVE

Perhaps a Year Later

Chapter 32

Sun lamps shone from the cavern roof upon pleasantly green terrain.

The lamps were powered by a small nuclear energy source. Once they had been switched on by the fleeing tribe, and once the roof sprinklers had delivered rain, the greening of the cavern floor had proceeded apace. All the pelleted seeds scattered across the sterile compost – lying till then in cool, dry darkness – had quickly yielded grass and vegetables, flowers and seedling trees.

For here was the late Bruno King's lavishly thought-out survival shelter, inherited by his avatar Ariel. It was a cavern measurable to man, but by no means cramped. It was a space colony: an asteroid ark buried underground. Bruno King had conceived it as this from the beginning, modelling its mechanics and ecology upon the dreams of the space colonization lobby, the High Frontiersmen, the L-Fivers. Those dreams, unfulfilled (as yet) in the world at large, had been realized here in secret beneath the uplands of the Farm.

Unlike any steel or stone eggshell in the sky (a species which still only existed in the imagination), this bubble in the Earth's crust came already equipped with gravity, and air, and radiation-proof walls. And with hot and cold running water. The air was pumped in through a filter system. The hot and cold H_2O rose from wells sunk to different levels. Yet the cavern was still a space colony – designed to sustain human life in a hostile environment for at least half a century. It was this in concept, if not in cost (though this hadn't been negligible). Only, its orbit lay not through space, but time.

Five stone temples were scattered about the cavern floor, miniatures of those up on the lost estate. For: as outside, so inside . . .

One temple enclosed a well-stocked library; a second held gardening tools; a third was a kitchen, built over a vault of canned and freeze-dried foodstuffs which came with a hundred-year guarantee – the suppliers, Survivalism Inc, being 51% owned by King Enterprises.

And the grass grew lush; and flowers bloomed; and saplings thrust towards the artificial suns.

As yet the only sizeable tree was Silvester. Now that he could no longer lure raw meat to fuel his ambulations (for there were neither birds nor squirrels in the ark), he had sunken his roots permanently. He grew near the banks of a stream flowing past the little Temple of Ancient Virtue, at a point where this stream broadened into a deep, clear pool.

Thus at last Silvester had become a fully-endowed tree. His legs had fused together to form a single trunk. Bark disguised his features now; extra branches sprouted from his shoulders. He had begun to stretch up and out. Yet he still retained the power of speech.

To celebrate the first anniversary of their descent underground, the tribe held a festival on the lawns of the Temple of Ancient Virtue.

To *celebrate* their exile?

Yes, indeed! For melancholy might creep over them in subsequent years, as one by one they died. (Not to be replaced by any changed children. During their flight, prompted by he knew not what, Ariel had electrically fused each person's spermatic ducts or fallopian tubes. Man had fitted out this cavern; and those who lived here were now beyond Homo: transhuman. Yet Homo would outlive them all . . .) But at this early stage in their subterranean life the tribe felt no pangs of nostalgia for the world they had lost. It was with gaiety and carefree verve that they celebrated: their release from the world and its responsibilities.

For Shetani, there were now no more terrors or shadows. The squashing of the chameleon-pig, which had been so very much a part of her, had spelled her liberation from it. Thus over the close-scythed turf she came, whistling a reedy tune.

And it was much the same with all of them who gathered there. Towards the surface of her pool Nixy swam slowly. Everyone present heard her voice rising thinly through the water, harmonizing with Shetani's melody; and though Nixy sounded far away at first, suddenly she was very close.

When she broke surface, Pan serenaded her with bamboo pipes which he had cut, himself. The lesser satyr handed the nymph's dripping person out of the pool quite gallantly.

Ariel glided down from the stone sky, like a true space-colony sportsman.

Geneva, long healed of her second Sansevieria wound and its attendant anguish, came over the stream in a single stride. She bore trusses of red tomatoes to the outdoor altar. In later years this altar would be curtained by a shady grove.

No disturbing photons pierced the cavern from outside, consequently Argus could far-see nothing that lay beyond. Yet those walls did not confine his vision; instead they freed it, inwardly. For now he saw the whole panoptic microworld of the cavern as a single living cell in perfect symbiosis with itself; and he felt at peace with it. Increasingly he would disguise himself as part of the local scenery, melting into the vegetable gardens, say. Today he carried courgettes and peppers to the altar, and these seemed to float through mid-air, guided simply by a mind. Whenever Argus happened to look into the past these days – and this was seldom – all that he saw was composed of folly and disorder and tyrannical ambition.

Even Silvester hummed, his barky throat vibrating.

Thelma led her tribe in an ode to joy, conducting them with her fingers and her toes . . .

> 'We all live in a fellow symbiosis,' they all sang,
> 'A fellow symbiosis,
> 'A fellow symbiosis!
> 'We all live in a fellow symbiosis . . .'

Today, instead of diving back into her pool with a cheeky flick of her rump, Nixy succumbed to the satyr's blandishments at last. Presently they retreated behind some bushes. Obligingly Thelma broadcast their raptures to the rest of the tribe, spreading their joy around to the embarrassment of no one.

Outside in the estate, singing was also in progress. There it was a sort of evensong, for daytime down in the cavern had drifted out of synch with daytime outside.

Reverend Drew Hayes presided at the service, hump-backed with the weight of moral duty, yet with two extra arms to help him bear such burdens. Robina Weber was by his side, dressed in a white robe. For they had just been married – feeling that they should not enact this sacrament in the full brightness of the day – and tonight was their unconsummatable wedding night. Consequently Robina wore white, which would never be stained by semen.

Drew Hayes was not of Thelma's (or Robina's) tribe, of course. Nor were several other members of the congregation. They remained unjoined: members of a potential, but now never to be, third tribe. Yet they were quite as convinced (by Gorgo) of the path to salvation, as any of the second tribe.

No one had demurred at Reverend Drew Hayes conducting his own marriage service; for the man was a tower of strength and inspiration to them. He had been tempted, and withstood – or so it seemed in retrospect. His sermon at the wedding had been on the theme of a medieval village which contracted plague. Resolved that the pestilence should not spread, the villagers had barricaded themselves away from the world, till every man-jack, and woman-jill, of them died out.

As for the marriage contract itself, this had only required minor changes. 'Will *I* take this Woman to my wedded wife? Not to have, and not to hold . . . ?'

Before the Temple of Venus, which was now the Chapel of Chastity, two score (and more) voices rose in song, to the strains of the Wedding March from *Tannhäuser*, yet with sterner words:

> 'We may not breed,
> 'Nor spill our seed:
> 'Till we have dried out,
> 'Then we'll be freed . . .'

Hayes squeezed Robina's hand in one of his additional hands.

'Soon as we get to Heaven, and get our proper bodies back, I'll make it up to you,' he promised.

Chapter 33

A little further off, in a walnut-panelled room with French windows, sat Reuben Maccoby studying a comic, as though somewhere in it lurked the real clue as to how he had succeeded so remarkably in life.

Bruno King's study had seen one notable change. House plants still crowded the rosewood harpsichord, which was suffering somewhat from drip stains and mildew. The cavemen on the wall still ambushed the doomed mammoth, since the picture hid the safe where Reuben now kept the company computer codes. But the book shelves had been cleared of all their abstruse tomes. Reuben had thought it best to have a bonfire of these, after burning all the lab records too. The empty spaces had by now mostly been filled up with long runs of comic books, many of them collector's items.

Pouring himself another shot of twelve-year-old Wild Turkey, Reuben thought how clever he had been. From bodyguard to boss!

But it didn't all quite add up.

Assiduously he scanned the ads in his copy of *Scare Stories*. 'Switchblade combs!' 'Whoopie cushions!' 'How many times have you felt left out?' 'Weight-melting anti-energy food!' 'Hypnosis lessons!'

Hypnosis? Lessons?

Reuben wondered why his head was starting to hurt. He wished it was Sunday morning, so that he could dial the religious programme on closed circuit. Sunday was a cleansing and rededicating day. So it ought to be.

One of the tales in this issue of *Scare Stories* told of a wicked French *Comte* who locked a brilliant philosopher in the dungeon of his château and starved him to death, to see how philosophical he would be about it . . .

For the first time in a while, Reuben recalled Ohira and Shiba, in their dungeon. He pressed his intercom button.

'Find McKinnon. Quick.'

When Carrot-Head came into the study ten minutes later, he did so without knocking.

'I don't think you knocked,' observed Reuben.

'Aw, come off it! You and me, Reuben, we're – '

Reuben held up his hand. 'There's gotta be respect.'

'Sure I respect you, Reuben. Anyone who could have pulled off all this . . . ! I mean, it beats me.'

The trouble was, it beat Reuben too. Which was why he couldn't afford to be too intimate with his old colleague. Actually, lots of things weren't allowed, and he had no idea why. Liquor was okay. And women were okay, just so long as he didn't bring them back to the Farm; which was a nuisance, since he had to be back on the Farm faithfully every Sunday morning to catch that programme on closed circuit.

And comics were okay, though some of the words fogged out occasionally. Words such as hyp . . . hyp . . .

Then there was the business of the Ace Detective Agency. If he had his own way (and why didn't he?), he would have sent Craig McKinnon on the trail like a bloodhound. Got rid of him that way. But it seemed that he had to keep McKinnon here, as his chauffeur.

It was always okay, so long as he didn't try to puzzle things out. His running of King Enterprises by remote control was, well, downright inspired. But it didn't add up, no sir.

And then at night sometimes he dreamed of the ground splitting open, and an imp flying out of hell straight at him. However, he only had to say a magic word, 'Egnach!' to send the imp scooting back into the abyss, screaming in frustration. He was in charge; not it. At other times, when he was awake, he couldn't pronounce the magic word.

'You want me to stand about all night like a dummy?' McKinnon asked peevishly.

'I'm *thinking*.'

Immediately McKinnon looked respectful; because whatever Reuben Maccoby's thoughts had been in the last year or so – and Craig couldn't fathom them – they had certainly brought the man to power. And even if Reuben hadn't cut Craig in on all the action, there were ample pickings.

'Those two doctors . . .' Reuben began thoughtfully.

'You want to see a doctor?'

'Shut up!' The very notion sent a shaft of migraine through Reuben's lobes. 'Them? They're no better than if they did experiments on Jews in prison camps. Trying to breed freaks and monsters.'

'Uh? They aren't that old. Well, maybe Ohira is. Those guys don't always show their age – different kind of skin, I guess.'

'We gotta keep them out of circulation forever, Craig.'

Was Reuben delivering a broad hint? McKinnon smiled slowly, as in the old pre-King days, to indicate that he had got the message. If message it was. To his astonishment Maccoby recoiled.

'No! Thou shalt not kill! What I was getting at, dummy, was an . . . an analogue. It's as *if* they're Nazi doctors, and we've caught us a couple. Governments are soft and sloppy, and would let them go.'

'But surely Japanese doctors never . . . I don't get you.'

'I suppose analogues are beyond you.'

'So okay. I never did understand computers.'

Maccoby stared at McKinnon in disgust. 'I want to check up on those two, personally. Right now – surprise inspection. Wily: that's what Orientals are. They could be scheming something.'

'You could easily patch the video through from – '

'I said personally. I don't trust TV.'

This, from the man who routinely locked himself in his study every Sunday morning, to goggle at a screen? McKinnon had watched Maccoby through binoculars, behind the French windows of a Sunday morning. That must be when Reuben did his real work of corporate decision-making. But McKinnon had never seen the screen itself. Wrong angle.

'We'll go visit them, us two. Maybe not *visit*, exactly. We'll spy from the gallery.'

'Whatever you say, boss.'

'That's better, Craig. Much better.' Maccoby rose. 'Off to the dungeons!'

'What dungeons?' asked McKinnon, perplexed. Immediately he spoke, he wished he hadn't. Probably this was another analogue. It was a sign of Reuben's superiority. This time, Maccoby was kind enough not to comment.

It was but a short distance to the former Chimporium, yet Maccoby insisted on being chauffeured there. By now it was dusk, and Reuben nodded approvingly when they were scanned by the guard in his glass cabin, while the Merc idled in the floodlit transit cage; though Reuben couldn't see whether or not the guard saluted. The mesh-gate rolled aside; the drawbridge descended; and the limousine purred onward. No sign, in the failing light, of any alligators. Or was that hump, on the bank of the moat, a pile of them?

Reuben keyed the intercom. 'Do you ever come and toss them steaks, Craig?'

'Who, Shiba and Ohira? I don't think they'd appreciate it, boss.'

'The alligators, lunkhead.' Yet there had seemed to be a note of guile in McKinnon's voice. 'They *are* getting fed properly?'

'Best porterhouse, honest.' Actually, McKinnon had a little arrangement worked out. The alligators were receiving offal: loads of lights and ox-liver, sweetbreads and heart. They didn't seem to notice any difference, gulping it all down. McKinnon wasn't particularly worried. He had been to Britain once, where he noticed butchers selling pig and lamb offal to people as though it was real food. What was good enough for the British was probably good enough for alligators.

'Hmm,' said Maccoby, making a mental note.

But already they were at the horseshoe. Reuben waited for McKinnon to hop out and hold the door for him.

A guard sat in the observation room, reading a girlie magazine.

Down below in the floral crater, underneath a bunch of green bananas, sat the two Japanese gene-doctors playing some game using ivory pieces marked with squiggles. They looked philosophical.

'They getting enough exercise? They ever work out on the bars?'

The guard shook his head. 'But they do some sort of slow dance routine every morning. For an hour or two.'

'You'd better watch that,' advised Maccoby. 'That's Chinese boxing. It's a martial art. You speed that dance up, and you become a lethal weapon.'

The guard patted his pistol, and smiled. 'Rest of the time, they sit and meditate. Or play games. Or – '

'Listen, boy: all those oriental games are *strategy* games. That's how they plan battles.'

'We never have to go in. They do their own gardening.'

'You'd better remember: four *chimps* once escaped from here.'

'Everything's under control,' McKinnon said soothingly. 'You can rely on me.'

Maccoby stared at his former partner, wondering whether this was a broad hint. He nodded – and deleted his mental note about the nourishment of alligators. There were times when a commander-in-chief ought to be flexible.

'You want to speak to them, boss?'

'Speak? Naw . . . People talk too much. The word, from now on, is "hush". Strength is silence.'

The word, actually, was 'Egnach'; but Reuben couldn't pronounce it, except when he was asleep.

Down in the Chimporium, the only sound was the faint click of a mah-jong tile. This was about the three hundred and fiftieth game that Ohira and Shiba had played.

Chapter 34

Still further away, in a curtained motel bedroom, a suitcase of money lay open on a bed. Mentamorpha eyed it.

'I *am* going to be an actress,' she said defiantly. 'That's final.'

'You mean, find somebody *real* who fits the part, and copy them? That isn't acting. That's cheating. Anyhow, what happens if you get to audition for a murderess? Or somebody haunted by infinite evil? Or the Queen of Atlantis? Where are you going to find one of those walking down the streets?'

Prote wore the middle-aged body of a bank manager from a hundred miles back along their route. He ought to have changed it by now, but they had left the previous city in rather a hurry, so he was still stuck in the same male flesh.

Mentamorpha tossed her head. 'That was dumb thinking on my part. I don't need a real-life prototype to copy. All I need to do is copy the mind of a classy actress – then *I'll* be an actress too.'

'Sure, then you'll have glossy photos of you stuck up everywhere. You may be the brains of this outfit, honey, but you're way off track on that one. Publicity is the *last* thing we – '

Prote parted the curtains slightly again.

'Anyway, it's all irrelevant. There's a blue Ford parked over there. I've seen it before. Front wing's buckled. And I've seen the guy at the wheel. He was in Berryford. He's been sitting watching for twenty minutes.'

'A cop?'

'Don't think so. He was just watching us in Berryford, too. He followed us on. He doesn't care if we play Bonny and Clyde, just so long as he can stick to us.'

'Government agent?'

'Hardly! It's got to be someone hired by the new Farm management, right? Now that I've spotted him, we can shake him. Here's where he loses the scent. But we'll have to act right away. Otherwise a back-up team could be on the way.'

'You *are* telling me the truth? You aren't just trying to turn me off my acting career?'

'Copy my mind. See for yourself.'

'I don't want to copy your mind. You know if I did that, we couldn't stick together. Or if *you* copied my body, Prote. It would be a sort of violation.'

'I'm telling you the truth all right! And now I'm slipping out the back way, to find a woman to copy.'

'Any damn excuse!' Mentamorpha stared disconsolately at the unslept-in bed. 'And here was me thinking we were going to have a little *fun*, while you're in that body. I'm not a fucking dyke, you know. I'm sick of sleeping with one damn female after another!'

'Honey, I promise you, once we're far enough away I'll find some really neat man to copy. You can pick him out yourself. I'll give you a fun weekend.'

'A fun *fortnight*.'

'A week.'

'Ten days.'

'No, damn it, a week.'

'Just get packed, will you? I'll rent us a new wagon. We'll drive to the nearest airfield and hire a private plane. We can afford it. Then we'll hop jets for a while. That'll shake our bloodhound for the next year or so. I guess it was plain bad luck him finding us. But it could be our fault, a bit. We haven't been looking over our shoulders enough. We've been moving too slowly. We'll pull a few big jobs then head abroad. How about the South of France?'

'Cannes!'

'No, *not* the Cannes Film Festival. I was thinking more of Monte Carlo. We could be a winning combination. Then we'll travel right round the world. Wouldn't you like to be able to think in Hindi and Chinese? Wouldn't you love to have Indians and South Sea Islanders tumbling in the sheets with you?'

'Hey, that sounds interesting.'

'And if we're right round the other side of the Earth, we won't have this nagging sense of old Thelma plucking at us. The scene *they're* in, I don't want to know about, however neat it seems to them. We'll put a bit more inverse square law between us and the Farm.'

'Couldn't it be Thelma who sent that man?'

'What, Thelma co-operate with Robina? You know our tribe are all bottled up. Thelma's the genie with the light brown hair. She's stuck in a bottle. And they're all very happy in it, thank you. Look, I'll be back in an hour. You be ready, hmm?'

'Ready for another woman.'

'I'll copy an old woman this time. I'll be a mother to you.'

'My Mom wasn't old! How old do you think I am?'

'*Sorry.*'

'Forgiven!' Impulsively, Mentamorpha rose and kissed the bank manager. Her tongue slid briefly into his mouth, and she pressed him to her. After a minute, Prote gently disengaged himself.

'That was sweet of you.'

'Just saying goodbye to my man,' said Mentamorpha wryly.

She hauled a second suitcase from the baggage stand, dumped it on the bed, then began tossing clothes from the closet in its direction, clothes which she had hung up half an hour before.

Chapter 35

In Shiloh, Reverend Jake Hogan inspected his face in a washroom mirror. That granite countenance betrayed a few cracks, product of the assault on him by the forces of Demoniacal Corruption. Occasionally his lip wobbled, and his left eyelid was smitten with a tic. But his hair had been white before the event, so no change was noticeable there. Divine guidance, a devout doctor and drug therapy had rallied him within a few months of the terrible affair. All in all, he had made a remarkable recovery. Apart from the tic and the wobble. He felt quite chipper enough to chair the forthcoming get-together of the Righteous Regional Apostles of the Conclave of Christ.

Leaving the washroom, he strode along the corridor to the Holy Family's boardroom.

Item two on the agenda, after Prayers, was whether to confirm Reverend Matt Bryson as Regional Apostle in Pompey. Reverend Bryson had been Acting RA since a week after the incident. So he too was present that evening at the cross-shaped table. He was a young charismatic, with intense dark eyes and sleek black hair which he wore oiled. Ladies adored him. He dressed all in black and looked like an old-world Jesuit confessor to royal families.

'I guess the meeting ought to ask you to step outside while we discuss this one,' said Jake. He scrutinized the maroon leather of the tabletop, waiting for Bryson to murmur and withdraw.

'Hang on,' said Reverend Chip Bannerson. 'On a point of information, oughtn't we to hear formally that there ain't no more update on Drew Hayes or the two Trinities that went missing? Before Matt scoots.'

The meeting agreed.

But no, reported Bryson, nothing more had been learned beyond what they already knew; which added up to an overwhelming enigma.

'Unless,' added Bryson, 'it's negative information. Whatever was going on has died down flat. They're as quiet as mice on that funny farm of King's.'

'And that's since Reverend Hayes vanished,' observed Reverend Joel Harkins. 'Coincidence, d'you suppose? Or cause and effect?'

'What are you getting at?' demanded Jake. 'You can't surely be suggesting . . . I *knew* that man like a brother!'

'Like Abel knew Cain?'

'Okay, so when I last saw him, he'd changed.'

'In what way exactly?' asked Harkins.

'I don't know . . .' Jake didn't quite want to think about this.

'So how do you know he'd changed?'

'He didn't seem to know who he was. Or who I was.'

'Let's be fair,' said Chip Bannerson, 'you were pretty disturbed round about that time.'

'Not before I went to Pompey, I wasn't! It was only when . . . when

I saw . . .' The dog with a human head. The whore. The living chair. No one had quite believed Jake at the time. Now, a year later, at times he wondered whether he had been the victim of a hallucinogenic drug. Or had he been vouchsafed a vision? Like Saint John the Divine? But if it was a vision, what sort of vision was *that*? A grotesque one! A hellish one! And if it was indeed a vision or a drug fugue, why had Drew Hayes genuinely disappeared afterwards? It didn't make sense. The whole episode had been absurd. More like an obscene version of the Keystone Cops than the Book of Revelations. Jake Hogan shook his head.

Reverend Chuck Wilson drummed his fingers on the table. 'Occurs to me, fellow Apostles, that we are one Apostle short.'

Jake rallied. 'So we should get on without further ado, and vote on Matt's promotion.'

'Ain't quite what I meant. We're one short, and so were those other Twelve Apostles, after Judas did his dirty deed. And the name of the Apostle they elected in Judas's place – '

'Was Matthias,' said Harkins. 'Matt, for short.'

'So,' went on Wilson, 'the question is: was Drew Hayes a Judas man? Had Satan gotten to him?' He gazed levelly at Jake. 'The dog with the human head.'

'No, no, nonsense.' Jake recoiled from this prospect. 'The Devil doesn't really – '

'Really what? Really intervene in human affairs directly in the twentieth century?' Reverend Wilson licked his lips. 'Soon as you lose your belief in the Devil, that's the first step on the road to A-thee-ism. Next thing, you lose your faith in Christ.'

Jake could feel his eyelid twitching. What had happened in Pompey a year ago had been totally absurd. He thought he had come to terms with it. Now he was being asked to declare his faith in the absurd – which no one had really seemed to believe in at the time! Just when he had gotten over it. To proclaim the absurd, in order to proclaim Faith! Didn't that make Faith absurd, too? 'I believe, because it is absurd . . .' Some saint had said that, in Latin. He could feel his position and foundations slipping away.

However, Jake Hogan was a man of granite, not soft clay. He had improvised enough times in the past, mainly sermons. Obviously now was the time for a flash of the old genius, which had been dormant for the last year. He thought furiously.

Then he gripped the edge of the table, and favoured the meeting with his best piano keyboard of a smile.

'Yeah, you're right, Chuck.' Jake's ivories flashed. 'But people ain't *losing* faith in the Demonic. They're gaining it. Look at all these devil movies in the last few years: these *Exorcizers* and *Presages*, and *Slitherings* and *Shriekings* and things. We've inveighed against them. We've put pressure on movie theatres and TV networks. But that was dumb.

'I've been thinking.' He had been, too. 'And I'm gonna propose under any other business that the Conclave of Christ oughta put money into a movie of Devilish Horror – but not officially or publicly, if you take my point. This movie'll feature a Righteous Ranger team, or even maybe somebody acting the role of a Regional Apostle. It'll goddamn well *scare* people to see the light, for their souls' sake. In a word, literally, we'll give 'em hell!

'You gotta know how to *use* the media, boys.'

He sat back. 'That's the pious proposal. Under any other business, of course.'

The other Regional Apostles, and Reverend Bryson (deputizing), stared at Jake.

'So now can we get on with Matt's election?'

But the meeting continued to stare at him. After a while, Jake's lips started to wobble.

Chapter 36

In their well-appointed, air-conditioned quarters on the air base, Cleo sat herself down at the keyboard and typed, in lower case:

much wisdom we can show you. not details of the star drive. no. our pilots are both dead in the crash. we are four students who study other worlds. but we are sad. we have had our sex organs cut. this is standard procedure, so that we do not breed during the long journey. can you repair us?

The words glowed green on a big display screen. After scanning the communication, Major-General Howard E. Goodman stroked his steel-blue chin.

'Are you *sure* you're from another star system?' he asked. 'I mean, your genotype and blood sure seems astonishingly like Earth chimpanzees.'

Cleo exchanged swift hand signals with Brutus. The civilian speech therapist, fluent though he was in sign language, still couldn't make head nor tail of these alien hand-signs.

Cleo typed again:

we are from another star, yes. but we do not know star maps. we are not steersmen. so we cannot point to it. our star is blue. our planet is number five.

'What do you know! That could *just* be Vega!' cried an excited voice. The civilian astronomy consultant from the local university, Dr Herschbinder, had long been a partisan of the idea of alien intelligences dwelling out in the cosmos. 'That's one of the closest candidates: only twenty-seven light years. Vega's a brilliant blue.'

'Why?' asked Goodman. 'Why's it blue?'

'That's its spectral class. It's fifty times as powerful as our own sun.'

'Isn't it kind of hot there?' said Goodman suspiciously. 'So what do they need those fur coats for?'

'Ah! Well . . . Earth is the third planet from *our* sun – but their planet is number five from Vega. It's further away. That would put it somewhere out in our asteroid belt, where our own fifth planet was originally. The planet Phaethon.'

'The what?'

'Phaethon. It exploded. Maybe there was a civilization there, and they destroyed themselves in a terrible war. Half of Phaethon got blasted into asteroids, Major . . . uh, General, and the rest raced off towards Saturn. It lost one of its moons there, which broke up into the Rings, then zoomed on to Uranus. It pulled a slice off Uranus – which slapped back down again, knocking Uranus sideways on its axis. And the rest of Phaethon ended up as Pluto . . . Mind you, that's just a *theory*. But it's a reasonable one. Fits the facts. So you see, Vega is a whole lot brighter, but their planet orbits further out.'

'Uh-huh. In that case, wouldn't they like blue light in here?'

'Well, when I say "blue", it isn't *just* blue if you're out there in person. It's blue-white. Or white-blue. Bright, though. Bright as Einstein. Maybe you could increase the light intensity in here; but then maybe us humans would all get headaches.'

'I already have a headache. Four, in fact.'

'So you see, you'd have to wear tinted shades if you went to their world, General . . . uh, Major,' said Herschbinder.

Distrusting the drift of this conversation – in case she and her friends should be blinded by blue arc-lights – but forewarned now about Vega and bright suns in general, Cleo hastily typed:

we tell you all about our planet. history. legends. geography. social arrangements. poetry. plants . . .

This would require a lot of co-ordinated improvization, and keen memories too; but Cleo felt that the four of them were up to it. She thought of Dr Herschbinder's planet Phaethon, wrecked by smelly bombs.

we tell you how we avoided destroying ourselves in war. but not much hard science. not our field. in return, can you please repair our sex organs?

'Why?' asked Goodman. 'What's special about getting them repaired?'

we apply for asylum. poor castaways, we. you receive much fruit of data in return. we teach you shreshmish.

'What's that?'

shreshmish is the alien mind skill of living together without fucking each other up. we can only show shreshmish if our sex organs are whole.

Cleo wondered for a moment whether it had been entirely a bright idea to turn themselves in. Yet the previous year spent skulking and scavenging around the fringes of human society had not been a huge success. The four of them had all lost weight. Caesar had become quite ill; his hair had started coming out in tufts. Boa had been bitten by a dog, and still limped on account of a severed nerve in her ankle.

Noting that Cleo's body had tensed up, and scenting the strain she

190

was under — though the dull humans noticed nothing of the sort —
Brutus decided to intervene.

He reached into a fruit bowl on the table by him. He selected. He
sniffed and bit the fruit in question. Ambling over, he waved it
appreciatively at Major-General Goodman. Leaning over Cleo's
shoulder, he typed:

very nice earth food. whats its name?

Goodman turned back from the screen, to Brutus. Patiently, he
explained:

'That's called a banana. Ba-na-na. But you aren't supposed to eat
the skin. You ought to peel it. Here, I'll show you how.'

Striding to the fruit bowl, Goodman snapped off a second banana.
He unzipped it, and took a demonstration bite.

Brutus pulled the remaining skin from his own banana and
dropped the skin, innocently, on the floor.